Nights in the City

A Temptation Press Anthology

NIGHTS
in the
CITY

A Collection of Steamy Tales

Nights in the City

A Collection of Steamy Tales

A Temptation Press Anthology

© 2020 Temptation Press, et al.
An Imprint of Zimbell House Publishing
Published in the United States by Temptation Press

This book is rated for 18+

All Rights Reserved

Trade Paper ISBN: 978-1-64390-131-2
.mobi ISBN: 978-1-64390-132-9
ePub ISBN: 978-1-64390-133-6
Library of Congress Control Number: 2019956730

First Edition: January 2020
10 9 8 7 6 5 4 3 2 1

Acknowledgments

Temptation Press would like to thank all those that contributed to this anthology. We chose to showcase five new voices that best embodied our vision for this anthology.

We would also like to thank all those on our Temptation Press team for all their hard work and dedication to these projects.

Table of Contents

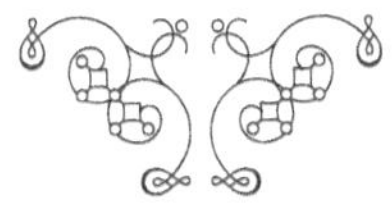

Chimera

Philippe Marron

I search for swingers clubs on my phone while we sit in traffic on the Golden Gate Bridge. Mia sleeps beside me. She, therefore, can't chastise me for not keeping my eyes on the road. One club only admits couples—no single men. I close the tab. I keep searching, one eye on the road. Sexual fantasies are a funny thing. They operate in an elusive, other universe. You have this thing that turns you on so much it can sometimes eclipse everything else, including healthy relationships and public safety. But this thing, this ideal scenario, is a chimera: irresistible and likely unachievable. The allure of sex clubs is that they promise at least the possibility of fulfillment. I scroll the reviews for another club. One reviewer described it disdainfully as a "sausage fest."

I glance at Mia and begin formulating my pitch.

In porn's parlance, the closest approximation to my fantasy is what is often described as a cuckold fetish. I enjoy imaging my girlfriend with other men. Sometimes, this takes on the scene of a full-blown gang-bang, with Mia flat on her back, legs spread, and a line of men leading out the door. More often, it's just me and another guy taking turns. He spends the night. In the morning, I use the bathroom and hear Mia giggling and then her rhythmic moans. Sometimes my fantasy is more nuanced. I imagine daytime trysts. She comes home flush from sex. She lost her underwear. Her pussy is sopping with another man's cum.

On the bridge—meaning, back in this universe—we're nearing the end of a nearly two-week camping trip. This was a major concession for her, someone who refers to herself as an "indoor cat." Now dirt smudges her cheek and her knees. She smells like a campfire. Her clothes are disheveled. She looks at peace and radiant, but I know she'll never consider attending a sex club without a shower first and a good meal. Another funny thing about fantasies is that no two are exactly alike. Mia actually craves being the center of attention, but not in a lurid sense. She might surrender herself to a soccer team, but only for the players to adore her. I breeze back to our Airbnb in the Mission, thinking about where our sexual Venn diagrams overlap.

She stretches her long limbs as I park the car. "Mmm, are we there?"

"Yes." I kiss my fingertip and place it to her chapped lips.

"I dreamed we were lost in the woods."

"Well, we're back in the city now—our last night in California. I have a proposal for you, but I want to tell you about it after dinner."

Her eyes brighten. "No, tell me now! Pleeease?"

"Well, I think we should shower and eat a nice dinner somewhere. Then, we should go buy you a new dress and some nice shoes."

Her smile spreads nearly from one ear to the other. I feel a pang of cognitive dissonance. I love this woman, who I've been with now for three years. I'm luring her to a place where I hope to watch her have sex with strangers.

Reality and fantasy grind past one another like tectonic plates.

"I wanna take you to a swingers club," I say, carefully watching her face. To my relief, she doesn't stop smiling. She seems amused. "Nobody will know us there," I continue. "We don't need to have any expectations or anything. We can just go and check it out. No pressure. Worst-case scenario, it's lame, and we'll have a good laugh about it afterward. What do you think?"

"For you."

"You'll go?"

"Yes."

We carry our camping gear inside and pile it beside the twin bed. The Airbnb is a studio with a small bathroom. I wait on the bed while Mia takes a bath. I think back on the trip, the hikes, the sunsets, the amazing things we experienced together. Mia is an incredible woman: beautiful, patient, adventurous. I am without a doubt the luckiest man alive. I've done a lot of thinking about why the thought of sharing her with other men turns me on so much, and I've come to the conclusion that it's a subconscious way for me to coopt my fear of losing her, by turning it into something sexy. The wires in my brain that spark sensations of jealousy and arousal are inextricably wound together. By encouraging her to "stray" in a safe environment, I retain control. Other men can have their way with her if she chooses; only I get to take her home.

She emerges pink and clean from the bathroom, a towel wrapped around her torso. She then lifts the towel, revealing a cleanly shaved pussy. "Do you think the boys will like it?" she asks with an impish grin.

I'm so hard I could pound a tent stake into the frozen ground. She always knows exactly the right thing to say to drive me insane. I throw her to the bed. I hold her legs apart. I lick her lengthwise, just once. Her skin feels hot from the bath. She tastes clean. I want to make her come. Instead, I lick her one more time and then roll off the bed reluctantly.

"No, wait!" She tries to hold onto my shoulders. "Fuck me, pleeease!"

"We've gotta save it for tonight. If things go right, we're going to have a lot of sex later."

She pouts but otherwise doesn't argue. I take a shower. It feels great to watch all the grime swirl down the drain. My body feels toned from all the hiking. This is going better than I expected. Mia actually seems into the sex club. We've talked about our fantasies before, of course, but only as bedroom talk leading to otherwise monogamous sex.

For example, as I'm unbuttoning her blouse, she sometimes says, "You won't be the first one inside me today." It's not true, but she knows it's what I like to hear.

"Who was he?" I ask, kissing her neck, her earlobes.

She tilts her head in that lovely way that women do when their necks are kissed. "I don't know. I didn't ask for their names …"

She tells stories of how she was seduced, usually putting her spin on the fantasy. The men are always devilishly good-looking. She never intends to give into them, but they win her over. They lift her atop pedestals. They fawn over every inch. They tell her she's the most beautiful woman in the world. She melts in their hands. She relents, allowing herself to be passed around like a coveted toy. She can't help herself. Throughout our foreplay, she works me into an almost unquenchable desire with this filthy talk, until I ravage her. But this banter has never included plans to actually follow through with our fantasies. The swingers club will be our first step onto that rickety bridge between fantasy and reality.

When I come out of the shower, Mia is at the mirror putting on makeup for the first time in two weeks. She chooses a flamboyant orangey lipstick. She goes heavier than usual on the eyeliner. When she puts on her last clean camping outfit, she looks like a slightly whorish Girl Scout. I like it, but I resign to buy her a new outfit before dinner. I know she'll feel sexier in a dress. Also, dresses are way more fun to take off than flannel and hiking boots. As for me, I'll attend the sex club looking like a hipster lumberjack, my standard look: tall, tattooed, and slightly grizzled.

We walk out into the Mission, where cute boutiques abound. Mia is in heaven. We go to a dozen places. She tries on countless outfits—strapless, backless, halter dresses—strutting from changing rooms with her cheeks sucked in, an exaggerated *Vogue* expression, before twirling on her heels and arching her eyebrows, as if to ask, "What do you think of this one?"

I am of no help. She looks amazing in everything. She would make any model blush in comparison. Still, she rejects everything I pick out for her: too short, too low-cut, too slutty.

"We're going to a sex club," I remind her.

"I don't care. I'm not dressing like a whore."

We ultimately buy her two outfits: one for the club and another just because. On tonight's menu is a red, shift mini-dress with calf-high boots. She wears this out of the store, and I see heads immediately turning in her direction. By this point, we are both famished. We drop off the excess clothes back at the Airbnb and walk arm in arm to a nearby tapas restaurant.

Our server can't keep his tongue in his mouth. Mia is beaming. I order a bottle of Rioja. We feed each other croquettes and olives. The calamari is to die for. When we're nearly finished with the wine, without me asking, she reaches under the table and removes her panties, which she hands to me. I stuff them in my pocket. Again, she always knows how to make me crazy.

"I'll do whatever you ask tonight," she says. "Just remember to consider what I want too. I'm not just your manic-pixie-dream-girl."

"If you're not feeling it, we'll leave—absolutely no pressure. I love you."

"I love you too."

After dinner, we hail a rideshare to the swingers club, which is downtown. The driver, one of those ubiquitous San Francisco hipster types, chats nonstop. He can barely keep his eyes off my girlfriend. Tipsy from the wine, she chats back amicably. I suspect she's into him too. It's chilly now. I notice goosebumps on her arms. I rub them to warm her up. She doubles over laughing at something he says. I kiss the nape of her neck. She snuggles against me. I surreptitiously slip my hand up her dress just as we pull up to the swingers club. We thank the driver and walk to the club, which is lit up with a neon sign in the front.

A beefy bouncer with a shaved head checks our IDs and asks, "Do you know what this place is?"

We assure him we do.

"Good. No phones allowed, so you gotta check 'em at the front."

He holds open the door. Mia enters first. It's dark inside. The walls are painted black. They rattle gently from the bass of loud music far inside the building. An older woman with huge boobs and blue eye shadow sits behind a counter. She slides a clipboard toward us. On the front page is a list of rules. Mia and I scan them together.

The rules seem reasonable: "No means no"—that sort of thing. The second page is a liability waiver. This page is scarier. One line says the club isn't liable in cases of sexual assault. I glance at Mia. Her eyes are as round as quarters. She giggles nervously.

I put my arm around her. "Remember, we have no expectations tonight. I'll keep you safe, and we can leave anytime—even now, if you want to. It's not a big deal."

"No, I wanna see this," she says.

We sign the papers and hand over our phones, which the woman drops into a plastic bin, handing me a token to collect them later.

"The main floor is open to anyone," she says, smiling at Mia, "but the upstairs is couples only. There are semi-private rooms off the main hallway. They're all stocked with condoms. Be safe, sweetie—and have fun!"

I lead Mia through a curtain and down a corridor with the semi-private rooms off to one side. The rooms have no doors. Each one has a different theme. One room has a giant dildo mounted atop what looks like a saddle. Another has a sex swing. Mia pauses at this room and studies the swing, which has a seat for reclining and stirrups to keep one's legs apart. The air smells of disinfectant. She arches her eyebrows, and we keep walking.

The music, now discernable as techno, gets louder as we pass the rooms, which are all empty. The hallway bends and then opens into a large, open space with mirrors and stripper poles along the far wall. Several TV screens display porn videos along the walls. One film shows two bleach-blondes with fake tits fisting one another. Couches arranged in little nooks dot the center of the room. A small bar sits off on the room's left. A staircase climbs up the rightmost wall, leading to the couple's only area. Besides the bartender and three men looming in different corners, the club seems completely dead, filled only by the music's incessant beat.

As we're ordering rum punches, another couple appears on a terrace above the bar that we hadn't noticed before. I touch Mia's shoulder and indicate she should look up, which she does. The woman wears one of those "schoolgirl" costumes, with a plaid skirt and white blouse. The man, barrel-chested and dressed in slacks, looks like a Marine. The schoolgirl subtly gyrates her hips to the beat, causing her skirt to swish. Without a signal, they disappear back into the couple's area. Mia and I claim one of the nooks on the ground level and sip our drinks. The three odd men leer at us, unmoving.

"What do you think?" I ask Mia.

"I don't find this place sexy at all. These guys are all creepy as fuck."

I study the three men more carefully. She's right. One runs his hand through a mane of greasy, thinning hair. He looks like a sex offender. Another is short, with bushy eyebrows and an unkempt beard. The last wears a hood.

Behold, I think, *the chimera of Greek legend: a lion, a goat, and a serpent, all formed to the same body, a fantastic dream—but in reality, hideous.*

As I study the men, I find myself wondering what they want. *Does the lion dream of being invited to a gang-bang in one of the semi-private rooms? Does the goat merely want to watch?* When you see someone at a place where you've never been, it's natural to assume that person frequents the place. But the timidity of these men makes me wonder if they, like us, are here out of curiosity. It occurs to me I am not much different than them. I'm taller, far better-looking. Unlike them, I brought a beautiful woman to the party. But, our sexual Venn diagrams probably almost eclipse one another's.

"Well," I say, "I know it's not what we came for, but let's go check out the couples' area."

She shrugs, and we traverse the stairs, hand in hand. The men's heads turn as we pass, but they make no effort to talk to us. The couples' area is revealed to us slowly and from the top down as we ascend. This room is much smaller, with another stripper pole and more porn displayed on TV screens near the ceiling. We enter into a single nook with multiple couches. The music remains deafening. I'm the first to notice the other couple: the schoolgirl bent over one of the couches with her skirt hiked around her waist, and the Marine behind her, his hands on her hips, pants around his ankles. Seeing them too, Mia hesitates for a half step. I gently tug her hand up the last three or four stairs. The other couple faces us as if this scene was staged for our arrival. I linger near the top and watch them fuck because it's obviously what they want. The woman's face contorts into that wonderfully suppliant expression women sometimes make when they're about to orgasm. She looks hot, but this scene isn't my fantasy. I don't want to have sex with a schoolgirl. I want to watch the Marine have sex with my girlfriend.

I then notice Mia has kept moving and is now swinging around the stripper pole. I hadn't seen her walk away. I join her and she gives me her best striptease. She writhes her hips and tosses her hair to the music. I watch appreciatively. She runs her hands along her body, accentuating every curve and valley under the dress's flimsy fabric. She then reaches beneath the dress and pulls her bra out through the sleeve. She spins the bra in circles and tosses it to me with exaggerated fanfare. It's red and lacy and bought for this occasion at one of the boutiques. I glance at the other couple and realize they've slowed down and are now watching Mia too. My girlfriend has an audience of admirers, which I know is what she craves. She found a pedestal. Her eyes are sparkling. Hands clutching the dress's hem, she looks at me and bites her lip, then flips up the front, reminding me she's not wearing any underwear.

I step onto the stage, slip my hand up her dress, and push her against the pole. She is sopping wet. I glance at the other couple, whose eyes are glued to Mia. For a moment, I imagine the Marine bending Mia over the couch. The image makes me hard. I kiss her neck and turn her head so that she's looking back at our audience. But then I glance at them too, and the fact that they're looking back at me deeply unsettles me. I begin to lose interest, not in Mia but in the present scenario. Performing in front of another couple isn't why I came. It's a poor substitute for my fantasy. I suddenly just want to get away, to be alone with Mia, to chalk up the swingers club as a failed experiment. Mia, however, is anything but unsettled. She is panting. Her pupils are dilated. She's so wet it's like dipping my fingers into a bowl of warm water.

"You wanna go downstairs, where we can be alone?" I ask, remembering the semi-private rooms.

She nods, straightens her dress, and we head for the stairs. I smile at the couple as we pass. The schoolgirl pouts. The main floor is still empty, save for the same wretched men, still huddled in their respective corners. Mia parades down the stairs and through the room without even giving them a glance. The lion gives me a hopeful look. I shrug, trailing behind Mia, still clutching the bra she tossed me during the striptease.

She leads us back down the dark hallway and into the room with the sex swing. We kiss beneath the entranceway. Then, she hikes up her dress, leans back onto the swing, and hooks the heels of her boots into the stirrups. Her shaved pussy glistens. She looks magnificent. I toss her bra behind the swing. I unzip my jeans and pull them and my underwear down to my knees. I am hard and ready to consummate this bizarre evening by fucking my girlfriend on the sex swing, but I pause for a moment to contemplate the beauty that waits suspended before me.

Behold, I think, *the embodiment of my fantasy: a ravishing woman, my love, her legs spread for me (and whoever else might walk through the door)*—only the parenthetical part is now just a fantasy. It's just the two of us now, and that is exactly how I want it. She is perfect. Everything is perfect.

With a hand grasping one of the swing's ropes and my other hand holding my cock, I'm about to tell Mia that I love her when her facial expression suddenly changes from unbridled lust to revulsion. I turn my head to find the three heads of the chimera lurking behind me. Mia quickly presses her knees together, but with her heels still stuck in the stirrups, this does little to cover her bare vagina because her butt juts out from beneath. She tries frantically to pull the dress down, but given its shortness and her reclined position, she merely twists in the air, completely exposed and vulnerable. The other men, like me, all have their cocks in their hands.

The snake licks his lips. "Mind if I go first?"

"I'm sorry," I say, "but my girlfriend and I would like to be alone. There seems to have been a misunderstanding." I consider shoving them out of the room, but given that we're all holding our cocks, this seems like it could make things even weirder.

"I ain't misunderstand you," says the lion. "You wanted us to come in here and bang your girl."

I open my mouth, about to respond that I wanted no such thing—not *really*—when I recall shrugging at the man as we passed by just a few moments earlier. Had I inadvertently given him and the others some tacit signal to join us? How else to explain why they are all here in the room with us now, obviously expecting to make their fantasies come true? As I consider my culpability, Mia manages to climb off the swing and shoves past us, mascara streaming down her cheeks.

"Wait, Mia!" I pull up my pants and push past the men into the hallway. I see Mia storm around the bend, out of sight. Then, remembering her new bra, I dart back into the room and snatch it from the floor before racing after her.

I sprint past the front counter when the woman there shouts, "Hey, don't forget your phones!"

I fish in my pocket for the token. I don't have it. It must've slipped out when I pulled down my pants. I frantically explain this to the woman, who, painstakingly slow, sifts through the plastic bin and passes me our phones as if she's doing me the biggest favor in the world. I stuff them in my pockets and rush outside.

"Which way did she go?" I ask the bouncer.

"Who?"

"The woman in the red dress."

He points to the left, and I sprint for a block in that direction, still clenching Mia's bra. I look left, right, ahead—don't see her—and then jog another block.

What have I done? I betrayed my lover's trust, I humiliated her, I put her in danger—all for the sake of a crass fantasy. I took her downstairs to be used, hoping she might relent to those repulsive men, knowing full well that wasn't what she wanted. I treated her like nothing more than a sex object—not like a person I deeply respect, like the woman I love, whose feelings I cherish, whose presence in my life I treasure more than anything. I trampled over the boundaries of her Venn diagram. I might have considered her desires or found her an audience worthy of her beauty. Instead, like a dolt on his cell phone in traffic, I allowed my fantasy to take precedence over our relationship. She was right to run away—I am a pig, my cravings vulgar, unworthy of such an extraordinary woman.

Not seeing Mia anywhere, I retreat a block, now winded from running, then circle the sex club's block. I check back with the bouncer to see if she returned. He shakes his head. I walk concentric circles around the club, poking my head into various bars and a Laundromat. I try to jam the bra into my pocket to look less like a weirdo, but it's one of those push-up types and won't fit due to the underwire. I ask the homeless men I pass whether they've seen a beautiful woman in a red dress. One tells me he saw her get into a sedan, which I find doubtful, but I still give him a couple dollars.

By this point, I am beginning to fear that something could have happened to her, but the thought is too terrible to entertain. I consider calling the police, but what would I tell them? After canvassing the neighborhood for almost an hour, I decide to catch a rideshare back to the Airbnb. Our flight is tomorrow morning, and all of her stuff is there. She must return eventually. First, I skulk back to the club, where I leave a note for Mia, apologizing profusely, asking her to call me so I know she is safe.

The whole ride back, I scan the streets for a red dress. I keep my phone on my lap and check it constantly. I stare at Mia's phone too, even though it's of little use. It's after midnight now, and both phones are inexorably silent. The lights remain off at the Airbnb. There is no sign she has been there. I toss her bra onto the bedspread and immediately fall beside it, fully clothed, panicked but exhausted. My fear of losing Mia has sucked all the life out of me.

I rest one phone by each ear. I stare at the ceiling in abject self-loathing for what seems like an eternity. Dark thoughts wrack my mind with guilt. I check the phones incessantly to make sure they have sufficient battery. When her phone's charge falls below twenty percent, I plug it in and then lie on the floor to be close to it, just in case. When sirens sound outside, I run to the window and thrust open the curtains. It's just an ambulance passing by. I flop back on the bed. I am a shell of the man I was yesterday. I have all the confidence of a dog waiting for his master to come home.

It is in this state that I fall into a fitful sleep, occasionally starting at irrelevant noises outside, until my own phone, just inches from my ear, chirps, nearly causing me to leap off the bed. I unlock the phone with teeth gritted tight, only one eye open, to find a text from an unfamiliar number:

Mia wants you to know she is okay.

My fingers spew a book's length of questions along with an impassioned plea for Mia to come home to me. I then delete all this and write a more guilt-ridden plea. I delete this one too. Instead, I call the number. Unanswered, my call goes directly to the voicemail greeting of a man named Jake. I hang up and call again. This call, too, goes to Jake's voicemail. I try three more times with the same result.

"Hello," I finally say into Jake's voicemail. "You texted me a few minutes ago that Mia's safe. I, um, really appreciate that. I've been so worried about her, you have no idea … Look, can you please tell her I'm sorry and that I love her, and then have her call me … Thank you."

I follow this with a text:

> Please have Mia call me.

I wait for five excruciating minutes until my phone chimes again.

> This is Mia. I'll come back tomorrow before the flight I made a friend.

My thumbs are furiously typing a response when she adds:

> BTW you're an asshole you made me feel cheap.

> Baby, I am soooooo sorry. Please come back to me. I love you.

There is no response. I pace the room. I type more apologies, more pleas. I delete them all. I said what I needed to say. The ball is in her court. I wait another five minutes, then ten, then twenty. I am a gorilla in a cage, seething with jealousy. There is no way I can remain in the Airbnb alone all night while Mia cavorts with her new "friend," Jake. I leave her phone plugged into the wall and shoot out the door.

Every flash of red—a streetlight, a brake light, a checkered scarf—makes me jerk my head. My legs carry me unthinkingly into a bar in the middle of the block. I flop into a corner booth, dejected. The bar is crowded. The music is loud but mellow. I rest my phone on the table and check to make sure its volume is set to high. The server asks if I'm okay. I resist the urge to pour out my soul. Instead, I tell him I'm fine and order a beer. When the beer arrives, I chug half of it in two gulps and stare at my phone's blank screen for what seems like an eternity.

Mia is right. I made her feel cheap. I neglected to consider the things that I know turn her on. She wanted to be admired and seduced—not objectified. I led her to the sex swing, secretly hoping to watch her get gang-banged. I treated her like a sex doll, like the mere means to my fantasy's fulfillment, instead of a person with unique desires.

I imagine her now with Jake. They are sitting close to one other in some bar. He is listening to her every word, attentive to her needs, plying her with drinks, making her laugh, patiently waiting for the opportunity to take her home. Has he touched her yet? I suck down the rest of my beer and swallow hard. It's almost last call. I order another beer, but before it comes, my phone alights with a new message—this time from Mia's phone.

It reads:

We're at the Airbnb come back but you have to be nice.

We're at the Airbnb? All the blood rushes to my head. The room spins. She brought another man to our room! For several moments, I am too stunned to move, but I finally come to my senses. I wave off the beer. I hastily pay the tab. I run the half-block back to the room without even realizing I failed to respond to her message.

When I get there, I find Mia's bra, the one I left on the bed, hanging from the outside doorknob. The lights are on inside, but dim. I stand on the walkway until my heartbeat slows to a manageable rate. I then dial the entry code and open the door to what would have once been a diorama of my cuckold fantasy.

My girlfriend and this man are lying next to each other on the bed, their foreheads almost touching. A sheet is pulled up to their necks. Her red dress lies in a heap on the floor beside our camping gear. I see their legs intertwined through the contours of the sheet. It would be impossible for two lovers to be any more snuggly. The way he looks at her is the look of someone who's in love, who soon will be, or who is very good at pretending. The way Mia looks at this man, Jake, is the look of someone who very much loves to be looked at in that way.

She pulls her eyes from his with apparent difficulty and smiles at me. "What took you so long?"

I am simultaneously more jealous and more turned on than I have ever been. I am jealous because I immediately intuit from my girlfriend's body language that I am at risk of actually losing her. Jake's eyes are like a drug to her. She's known him less than two hours, but she's already hooked. As if in confirmation, her eyes return to his, pulled by an insurmountable force, and they kiss as if I'm not even there. It begins as a mere brush of the lips, unhurried, almost incidental. Then, with glassy eyes, she parts her lips. He captures her mouth. She writhes beneath the sheets. They kiss hungrily as I stand at the foot of the bed, my mouth open, dumbfounded. But my fingers, reflexively, undo the first two buttons of my shirt.

Most men in my situation, finding their girlfriend in bed with another man, would fly into a rage, storm out, or even commit manslaughter. Feelings of wrath, indignation, and vengefulness well in the pit of my stomach. I feel my heartbeat throbbing in the capillaries of my cheeks. The heat and pressure threaten to blow off the top of my head. But just as Mia is drawn powerfully to Jake's attention, my anger and jealousy are overcome by a different force, similarly irresistible: to let my girlfriend have her fun and then win her back. I finish unbuttoning my shirt and then unlace my boots. Mia's eyes turn to me as Jake chews on her lip. I sit on the bed to take off my jeans. She reaches over and lifts a corner of the sheet, inviting me in. I finish removing my clothes and climb in beside her.

The warmth beneath the sheets is palpable. Mia turns her body toward me. She seeks my mouth, and we kiss for the first time since the club. Her mouth is wet from kissing Jake. Our kiss is tentative at first. I feel no apprehension about what is happening, except I now desperately need to know she still loves me, so I kiss her searchingly. She tastes like whiskey. The room reeks of sex. I seek out her eyes, but they are screwed tight. She is a woman in rapture. This is her fantasy. She reaches for my dick. For a moment, I make eye contact with Jake behind her. He looks like my stunt double—handsome, bearded, pseudo-rugged.

"She said you wouldn't mind this," he says with a crooked grin.

Mia's hand finds my cock and gives it a tug. "He doesn't mind, I promise."

I am jealous beyond words, but my perversity is plain. I'm as hard as a wooden dowel. I break eye contact with Jake. I hook a hand around Mia's neck and kiss her hard. I desperately want my girlfriend back. I want to share her, it's undeniable—but I also want her all to myself. I reach between her legs and am surprised to find Jake's hand already there. He is reaching between her legs from the rear. His fingers, two of them, are deep inside her. Not wanting to cede this vital area to him without a protest, I join two of my fingers to his.

"You're not the first one in there," she says, stifling a giggle against my mouth.

I suck her tongue. Between her legs, I match his rhythm. Our slippery fingers slide in and out in unison. But being in the front, I've blocked his access to her clit. She moans and shudders as an orgasm builds, and I know I'm the one principally responsible for it. But then, inexplicably, she releases my cock and pivots again to Jake. I am left with her backside and my wet fingers. He takes her mouth. I no longer know what is happening beneath the sheets. She straddles him. She lifts her butt and reaches down between her legs. I can't see it, but I can tell she is guiding him inside her. If there was any doubt, she deliberately lowers her body, inch by inch, and her eyes roll back in a look of consummate bliss. His arms encircle her. He holds her tightly against his chest. She and Jake remain like this for some time, as deep and close as they can possibly be, their lips locked in a passionate kiss before Mia begins to grind her hips against him.

As I watch my girlfriend fucking this man, I'm a bystander, a voyeur—which is exactly what I've always craved—only now it's not enough. I love this woman. I know this with a zealot's assuredness. I love everything about her: her laugh, her imagination, her cleverness, her incredible beauty, her teasing sense of humor, her openness for adventures of all types. Even now, as she thrashes and moans against this stranger, I feel no anger. I wish her only ecstasy. I suddenly want nothing but to convey to her how perfect I think she is. I brush the hair from her eyes. I press my lips to her ear.

"I love you," I whisper. "No matter what happens, I'll always love you."

She turns her head, and our eyes meet. She is so blissed out I can't tell if she even heard me. She looks like an utterly beautiful, drooling idiot, like she's zonked out on the most euphoric drug imaginable. I peel back the sheet and run my hands down her back. Her skin shimmers with sweat. I reverently trace her svelte body all the way down the back of her legs. I kiss her ankles, her heels, the backs of her knees.

Meanwhile, she never stops writhing against Jake. He's obviously hitting her in just the right spot. As I plant kisses on the small of her back and along her waist, she fucks him harder, shamelessly, piston fast, clearly building to a phenomenal orgasm.

I return to her ear. I whisper again that I love her and that she is beautiful and perfect. I compare her to the mortal Psyche, who was so gorgeous as to incur the goddess Aphrodite's wrath. I stroke her hair and tell her everything is going to be okay. I may not be able to wiggle between this man and her clit—certainly not in this moment—but I have her ear, and I know her better than anyone. I tell her that her pretty face is never more splendid than when she comes and that I want to watch and then have her for myself, next, and then forever.

She turns to me with tears in her eyes, panting, "I love you, I'm sorry, I love you, I'm sorry …" in rhythm to the now desperate bucking of her pelvis.

Jake grabs her butt and pushes her down onto him even deeper.

"I love you, I'm sorry, I love you, I'm sorry, I love you …"

Positioned as I am off to her side, I witness the orgasm rock her body laterally in a way I've never seen before. The first shockwaves begin somewhere deep in her core. She moans like a woman who has lost all semblance of control. Her hips shake as if from an electric charge. She is drawn inward at first. Her knees and elbows involuntarily jerk toward one another—as much as the position allows them. Her hands clutch desperately to Jake's shoulders as if she might fall. The tremors then spread outward from her core, up her arms, down her thighs, encompassing her entire body. They carry her limbs outward, such that she lets go of Jake and clings instead to the sheets above his head. Her toes curl. It's a sight more magnificent than any natural wonder.

Whimpering, she slides off Jake and flops between us on her back, like a puddle of water. After a moment of catching her breath, she props herself onto an elbow and reaches for my hand. "We can ask Jake to leave now," she says, "if you want. He's a really nice guy, and he said all the right things tonight, but I'm yours, and I'll always be yours, as long as you want me."

I glance at Jake, whose dick is already going limp. I hadn't realized he had come too, or that they didn't use a condom. I was too focused on Mia.

"I'll leave," Jake says, climbing off the bed. "You're a lucky man."

I am an exceedingly lucky man. I cup one of Mia's breasts and let my hand glide down her stomach. She purrs at my touch. She still loves me. I'm the one who gets to hold this goddess in my arms tonight. I can make her my wife if I choose. I can keep her forever, as long as I treat her well and always consider her feelings. My confidence soars. I am Bellerophon, who slew the chimera. I'm no longer the least bit threatened by Jake, who, stooped to pick his clothes off the ground, no longer looks as tall or as handsome as I thought when he was fucking my girlfriend.

"You can stay if you want," I say to him, "assuming Mia wants you to." I slide my hand between her legs. I find her clit. "What do you say, my love? The two of us can take turns fucking you until daybreak."

She reaches for my dick again and pulls me on top of her. I'm ridiculously hard. She holds it pressed against her opening, where some of Jake's cum is beginning to seep out. "You next, and then we'll see," she says, biting her lip, eyes locked to mine. "But sure, Jake, you should stay the night with us. We can have some more fun until it's time to catch our plane."

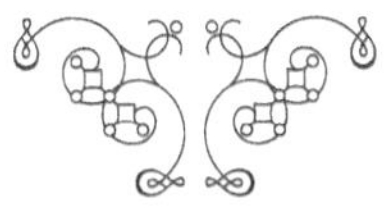

Her Dominant Ex

Shanjida Nusrath Ali

CHAPTER 1

INVITATION TO SAPPHIRE FORTRESS

Sapphire Fortress sincerely thanks you for joining our BDSM community through our website. You are invited to the Dark Pleasure Party on the
Fifteenth of January
6:00 p.m. at
36 Wyndham Street
Alexandria, NSW

RSVP by January 10 to sapphirefortress@gmail.com.

Dress code:
Men: White shirt with black suit and tie with matching shoes. Black/white Volto or Colombina mask.
Women: Black corset and lace panties with matching high heels. Black/white Volto or Colombina mask.

IMPORTANT: Must have invitation card and mask with you.

I read the invitation card for the fourth time. This was a stupid idea. *Why on Earth am I even doing this? To move on. Duh!*

Move on? Why not move on like a normal person? You know, spending the first four days in misery, drowning myself in ice cream and watching lame-ass— okay, not so lame-ass— romantic movies, knowing full well that none of that shit will happen in real life. Then, I would spend the next three days giving myself a pep talk about going out, not because I looked like a zombie, but because I had an actual life too. And finally, after another five days of hanging out with friends, going to a club and meeting new guys to get over your recent breakup is, of course, the next logical course of action. *Why not do that?*

Want an honest answer? Because you are crazy who wants to try crazy stuff. Normal is not your thing.

Hmm. True. And apparently, my subconscious seems smarter than me. Where was she when I was deciding whether I should go to go to the next level of my relationship with Alec? Oh, I know, the time I could have used some common sense, she hid like a coward in the corner.

And I still think it's a freaking stupid idea to go to an unknown place while half-naked for God knows how many people to see. *Ugh! Maybe I should just cancel it … or maybe I shouldn't? Fucking God help me.*

I glance up at the ceiling and huff in irritation. I look back to the floor-length mirror in front of me one last time, making sure I match the dress code for the party.

Black corset. Check.

Matching lace panties. Check.

Black heels. Check.

Smoky makeup. Check.

Invitation card and mask. Check.

I can totally do this. I can, and I will. I have had enough of hiding myself. Enough of trying to be something I'm not. It's time to discover myself tonight. I put on my coat and take the mask and card with me, locking my apartment door as I hail a cab to go to my destination.

It's time to find the new me.

CHAPTER 2

"Do you mind?" I tap my feet against the wooden floorboard, feeling irritated as the guy at the bar won't quit at it.

I arrived at the designated address like an hour ago. The guards at the door were pretty strict about the guest list, as they only let in the people who had the invitation card they received when they signed up on the online site like I did. The building looked like any normal nightclub from outside, but on the inside, it was a whole new world and extremely different.

It was a three-story building with the most expensive interior I have ever witnessed. The structure would probably fit my entire apartment building in it six times over. At both sides of the room in the corners, there were two long bar tables well-stocked with alcohol on the back shelves, and fancy-looking bartenders in black masks located on both sides. The vast, maroon-carpeted staircase was impossible to miss, as it led to the very interesting second floor. The whole floor had a total of seven rooms with a name tag on each one. They seemed more like themed rooms with names such as "Doctor's Appointment," "Internship Interview," "Strict Librarian," and "Detention Time."

But when I got to the final floor, I could not hold back my gasp. It was an entire floor filled with every BDSM item you could ever think of. You name it, and it's there. I knew I came here to explore myself, but I wasn't sure if I was ready for the heavy stuff. I thought everyone else would be just as nervous as I was, but it was quite the opposite. There seemed to be hundreds of people wearing black or white Volto and Colombina masks. The dress code that was mentioned in the card was worn as instructed.

After checking out the different floors and returning downstairs, two men dressed in full black suits and wearing white masks came into view on the second floor, grabbing everyone's attention. Both of them welcomed everyone and spent five minutes talking about the rules and regulations that should be followed. I swear to God, not even two minutes pass by after the men tell everyone to enjoy their night before half of the attendees start getting naked and start getting it on, as if they have been waiting for hours to start playing.

I won't deny that it was both shocking and highly arousing to watch the scenarios happening around me. Some guests were kissing or touching each other, starting things gently, and some even went to the upper floors to start their experience with their partners in the rooms. Then, there were those downstairs, who either danced to the music booming from the surrounding speakers, or they watched couples or groupies fucking each other from the barstools.

For a few moments, I didn't do much but walk around like a wanderer, taking in my surroundings. With every couple or groupie I passed by, I felt my breathing getting heavier, and I swear my panties were already getting wet from all of this. I wanted to join them badly, and I was sure they wouldn't mind at all, but for some reason, I just stood back and watched.

And now here I am, aroused and frustrated at the same time, while this douche has been annoying me with his cheap pickup lines.

"Is there a magnet in here? Because baby, I'm attracted to you."

I mean, really? Who even says that? I would have stopped this guy from the very start instead of giving a polite smile if I knew he was going to be so annoying.

"Do you mind?"

"Not at all," he slurs.

My eyes flicker over to the dance stage, where everyone is enjoying themselves, except for me. I look at the corner of the room and see the guards standing and scanning the place. I could go to them, but I don't want to create a scene.

"Let's dance," he says and grabs my arm.

"I-I can't. I'm waiting for someone." I stop him before he can drag me to the dance floor.

"You have been here for an hour, sweetie. No need to lie," he says, chuckling under his breath.

"I'm not lying. I am waiting for someone."

"Yeah? Who?" he asks.

God, will Mr. Creep give up already?

A tall, well-built guy with chocolate-colored hair walks past us, and I quickly grab him by the arm. He is wearing a black Volto mask, and I can see him frowning in confusion as he turns toward us.

"Him. He is my boyfriend." I smirk.

Mr. Creep frowns and curls his lip to check his opponent. My eyes scan the man I've just grabbed up and down. Even though he is wearing a mask, he looks freaking hot in that black suit with the top two buttons of his white shirt undone.

The guy looks at me, and his eyes flick back to Mr. Creep.

"And you are my ... girlfriend?" he questions.

"Yep." I nod. *God, please save me from this whole chaos.*

Mr. Hottie turns his gaze back to Mr. Creep and suddenly moves behind me as he snakes his arms around my waist, pulling me close to him.

Shit. I was trying to get away from one creep to only end up with another.

"Thank you for keeping my girlfriend company. Now, if you'll excuse us, I promised my girlfriend some fun time in the Doctor's Room," he says.

I narrow my eyes as I listen to his voice. *Why does he sound so familiar?* Before I can say anything further, he takes my hand, leads me out of the bar, and heads upstairs.

Woah! Are we really going where I think we are going?

"Um … Thank you for saving me, but I don't think you have to act anymore," I stammer, but he keeps walking until we reach the room with "Doctor's Appointment" written in bold, golden letters on the door.

He opens the door, and surprisingly, it's vacant. I walk inside and gasp. If a person comes into this room after seeing the name on the door, that person won't be disappointed at all. There is a desk, a bed at the center, a few utensils sitting on the side table, a doctor's coat on the desk, and a window overlooking the cityscape on the side.

I turn around and find Mr. Hottie leaning against the door, with his hands inside his pockets and legs crossed, as if the whole situation is casual. I was annoyed a few moments ago, but right now, I'm getting paranoid. *Why the fuck did I even come here in the first place?*

"I really didn't expect to see you here," he mutters.

"Well, you dragged me here."

He chuckles, and for some reason, the sound makes my body shiver in anticipation.

"I meant …" he says, walking toward me with confident strides until he is so close that there is only an inch gap between us, "I didn't expect to see you … here at this party, Viv," he whispers.

I move back immediately in shock. *What the …* only one person used to call me "Viv."

Alec. My ex-boyfriend. *What on Earth is he doing here?*

CHAPTER 3

"Alec? What are you doing here?" I ask frantically.

"Better question, what are *you* doing here?" he asks, taking a step toward me and revealing his mask.

My breath hitches. He is just like how I remembered: sexy, hot, and drop-dead gorgeous. He puts his mask on the desk before his beautiful, brown eyes meet mine, followed by a smirk on his face.

"I can be wherever I want to be. We broke up. Remember?" I cross my arms and narrow my eyes.

He rests his ass against the desk and mimics my posture by crossing his arms as well. "I remember many good things as well," he says as his eyes flick to me, scanning me before he smiles sexily.

I roll my eyes. "What?"

"Just imagining."

I raise a brow. "Imagining what?"

"How soft your skin will feel when I grab it while I'm fucking you."

My mouth drops open in shock.

He smiles a slow, sexy smile and points toward the bed. "Now, why don't you strip and we can start to play a bit?" he asks and takes off his suit jacket.

"Yeah, right. I'm going to pass," I say and walk toward the door.

"That loser might be roaming outside just waiting to get ahold of you again, you know?"

I stop with my hand on the handle. *Shit. He is right. But I won't give him the power to think that he is right. I can deal with that creep myself.*

"I can handle it myself," I say and unlock the door.

"Viv, get back here right now. Otherwise, there will be consequences," he says in a serious, demanding voice.

He has never used such a tone with me, ever. I lick my dry lips and feel my breath suddenly getting shallow. I feel him before I hear him walking toward me. When he stands behind me, I can feel his breath against the back of my neck, making my heart pound faster. He runs his finger along my arm, which sends goosebumps all over my skin.

"I noticed you walking around the whole time, Viv. You could have explored with anybody. There are countless volunteers, yet you didn't pick them. Why?"

I can't deny the truth this time. I have been wondering why I hadn't started anything with anyone. I don't think I know the answer myself.

He kisses my neck, his lips touching my pulse point. My eyes close in desire as arousal kicks in between my legs.

"Because you wanted to explore with someone who you can trust, someone who can make you feel safe," he states.

Maybe he is right.

"I can make you feel safe, Viv. I always will. I want to explore this new part of you with you," he whispers, biting my earlobe softly, making me moan quietly.

"I promise to take it slow with you, and if you still want to leave, then I won't stop you." With that said, he moves back.

I whine under my breath, missing his touch. I turn around, finding him near the bed as he rolls up his sleeves and takes the stethoscope from the utensil plate, putting it around his neck.

"Your decision," he says as he stands, waiting for my answer.

I know this is a bad idea. I can feel it in my gut, but he is not wrong. I do feel safe with him, and I do trust him. That's the first rule of BDSM: explore with a partner who you can trust and feel safe with.

With a sigh, I take off my mask and walk toward him. *God, why does he have to look so fucking gorgeous?* I swallow the lump in my throat and stand before him. He dusts his knuckles along my cheek, making my breath hitch. He feels so rough, yet so warm. So safe.

"Have you done your research?" he asks.

I nod.

"What are your hard limits?"

"No wax play, blood play, or fire play. No chains or wooden paddle. And absolutely no fisting," I state. I have researched thoroughly on Google, so I know what I want and what I don't want. He gives me a dark smile as if amused by my knowledge.

"And soft limits?"

"Anal play and gagging." I twist my hands while feeling more and more nervous about everything.

"Are you on the pill?" he asks.

"Yes, and I'm clean."

"So am I." He runs his thumb along my bottom lip and kisses my forehead. "You are safe with me. I promise. Let's have some fun."

I hope he knows what he is doing.

CHAPTER 4

Alec pushes up the sleeves of his white lab coat and turns to me. I am on the examination bed, naked and waiting. I'm not surprised that he chose the doctor's role.

After all, he is a doctor in real life working as a cardiologist.

"What's your name?" he asked, getting into his role.

"Vivian Susie Jameson," I reply as I try my best to get myself under control. It's really difficult with him making me feel so hot and bothered, and he hasn't even started touching me.

He smiled. "Patient is cooperative." He pretends to write something. "Now, why don't you tell me why you are here today?"

We didn't discuss anything about what to say or how to act, so I have no idea what he is going to do. Luckily, I have a limitless imagination, so it won't be a problem for me.

"My husband sent me here."

"I see, and why is that?"

"Well, it's been a long time since we have had sex, and when he showed me his huge dick, I wasn't sure if I could take him. So here I am, to make sure things are okay down there," I say, biting my lip, acting all innocent.

"You want me to see if your husband can fuck you?"

I nod frantically.

"Hmm … I may have to do a thorough examination."

I gulp and grab the bed sheet tightly. The promise that he holds behind those words makes every nerve in my body shiver.

"I don't mind."

"You don't mind if a stranger spreads your legs and touches every inch of your pussy?" he asks in a gruff voice.

I shake my head as my breathing gets heavier. He runs his warm palm along my thighs while looking down between my legs. He is nowhere near my pussy, and I am already getting wet. *Oh my.*

"Everything looks good from a visual perspective. Let's see how responsive you are," he says while running his hands up and down my legs, teasing me.

I wiggle, trying to get his hands closer to where I wanted to be touched. Out of nowhere, he smacks my inner thigh, and I yelp in surprise.

"Don't interfere with my checkup. I'm the doctor, so I know best," he warns in a serious tone, and something about it turns me on even more. *Who is this guy?*

He resumes his slow stroking as his fingers trail up and down, turning me on so much that I feel hypersensitive. "There you go. Look how turned on you are, and I've barely touched you."

I didn't say anything. I have no words.

"Aren't you?" he asked.

I closed my eyes, feeling his calloused fingers.

He smacks my pussy this time, and I can't help but let a loud moan out of my mouth.

"When I ask a question, I expect an answer."

"Yes, Doctor."

Satisfied with my answer, he runs a finger along my slit and circles my clit. My hips jerk slightly. "You don't seem to have a problem getting aroused, so that's a good sign. Now let's see how much you can take." He repeated this action a few more times before inserting his index finger inside me.

My whole body jerks as I moan with my back arched. *Oh, my God.*

"Don't move, just feel," he whispers as he pushes his finger in and out a few times before inserting a second finger.

I buck against him, and he forces my hips back to the bed. "Move one more time and see what happens," he warns, and this time, he leans down and tortures me with his mouth.

I scream out loud with pleasure overload as he sucks on my clit while fucking me with his fingers. He licks and nibbles, switching it up occasionally, and then adds three fingers. *Oh god*! This is too much. I have never experienced such action from him—ever. Alec was always a gentle lover when it came to sex, but this? Seeing this new side of him is blowing my mind.

He pulls back suddenly as if he knows I am on the peak of my orgasm. My legs tremble, but I do my best to follow his order to stay still. He unbuckles his belt and pulls down his zipper before his dick springs free. *Holy fuck*! It's been three months since we broke up, and I forgot how huge his dick was … or *still is*.

"Ready for your next test?" he asks with a smug smile on his face.

I nod my head.

He chuckles before cupping my face and leaning down to plant a chaste kiss on my lips. *God, I missed him so much.* We broke up for a reason, and yet I still couldn't stop thinking about him. His touch, his love, and his presence always kept running through my mind. I kiss him back, combing my fingers through his hair, biting his lower lip as his tongue traces my lips.

He leans back, resting his forehead against mine. "Trust me, you are ready."

Moving back, he strokes his dick, making my heart pound faster and faster. If someone could die just by seeing a man pleasuring himself, then that would be me. He slaps his dick a few times against my clit as I let out a groan. He lines himself up with my pussy, and, without any warning, he pushes straight in.

"Holy shit," I gasped.

He holds my jaw, drawing my eyes to his. "Such a bad girl for cussing so much," he grunts and continues fucking me with deep and hard strokes.

I clench with every hard push as I feel my insides tightening. I can feel myself coming already. He kisses my cheek and runs his nose up and down my skin while tightening his grip on me. Most people would have been scared by now, but with his dominance, I feel like I'm in seventh heaven.

"I can feel you coming already, baby. Come for me. Be a good girl and do as you are told," he orders.

And, as if a switch has been turned on, I come immediately just from his words. My orgasm takes over me as I cry out loud with my body shaking. When I catch my breath, I notice that he hasn't come yet, even though I did. I frown in confusion.

"You didn't come?" I breathe.

He shakes his head. "Not before I make you come three more times."

My eyes widen in shock. *Three times? That's impossible.* "But I—I," I stammer.

He shakes his head. "I control everything here. When I say you will come three times, that means you will come three times. You will do as you are told, won't you, baby?" he purrs and moves back and forth slowly, igniting my body on fire.

I nod, and my eyes roll back as I feel him everywhere.

He jerks my head with his hand gripping my jaw. "Answer me," he growls.

"Yes, Doctor."

"Good girl," he whispers and pulls out as I whimper with his absence.

He pulls me off the bed and turns me around, my back facing his front. He pushes me down by my shoulder as I rest my elbows on the bed with my back arched. I feel more vulnerable than I ever have before.

He drops his lab coat and kneels down with his rock hard dick still hanging out. I have no idea how he is even controlling himself.

"Let's see how you respond with my tongue on your sensitive pussy."

Before I can think any further about this idea, I feel his tongue immediately on my pussy. I gasp and grind myself on his face as he thrusts his tongue inside me.

"You taste so perfect, just how I remember, Viv. I could eat you out all night."

I wish he did. He licks and sucks and thrusts until my breathing changes and becomes frantic. He takes my clit between his fingers and pinches it gently, sucking me as hard as he can. And that's my undoing. I come so hard as I feel my insides spasm. My legs give out, and I almost collapse on the floor, but luckily, Alec is there to hold me.

He spanks my ass, making me yelp, then grabs a fistful of my hair, leaning my head back. He whispers in my ear, "Two more left. Now you better come with that fuckable mouth of yours on my cock."

My eyes meet his questioningly. We have been together for a long time, but I have never put him in my mouth. Don't get me wrong, I tried, but he never let me, giving excuses such as, "You don't have to do that," or, "I don't need it."

The Alec I'm seeing right now has been the absolute opposite of what he was when we were in a relationship. He was always sweet and gentle with me. I really loved that side of him, but I wanted to explore this new experience with him too. How I got the urge to want to try BDSM, I don't know. It's just whenever we had sex, I couldn't stop thinking about him tying my hands to the bedpost, or spanking me whenever I did something that pissed him off. I really tried the whole vanilla relationship with him, but in the end, I felt like I was missing something. I was too scared of telling him about my fantasies, though, and I was even more scared of him thinking I'm some sort of weirdo.

That's why I broke things off with Alec. But if I knew about this side of Alec before, then things wouldn't have ended so quickly between us. It was really hard for me to let him go, but because I loved him so much, I didn't want him to do something that I found pleasure in but made him uncomfortable. But why this sudden change? Why now?

CHAPTER 5

"Do it, baby, suck it, because when I come, it will be inside you," he says.

With no need for further elaboration, I kneel down as I look up at his handsome face and take him in my mouth. He tips his head back and groans. I start to suck him the best I can, but he's so big that he barely fits into my mouth. I slowly slide down his shaft, tasting him, and he presses me down further, holding the back of my head.

I suppress a gag as he slides into my throat. When I look up at him and meet his lustful, dark eyes, I can feel another round of arousal lighting up. *How can he make me feel this way?*

"Spread those legs and touch yourself, Viv."

His eyes roll back when I work up and down his cock, moving faster. I do as I'm told and touch my clit while sucking him deeper into my mouth. Pleasure rocks through me, and I can't believe I'm doing this for him, but it feels so damn good.

"That's a good girl," he whispers and strokes my hair. "You look so fucking beautiful, baby. Keep touching yourself until you come with my cock in your mouth, and then I will come inside you."

I moan with his cock between my lips. It comes out as a stifled noise when he thrusts further and hits the back of my throat. Spit drools down my chin, but I don't care. He pushes inside me with small, fast thrusts, making me speed up my fingers on my clit. And before I know it, I'm coming again with his cock in my mouth. My legs start shaking, but I hold on to his thighs for leverage.

He takes me by the hair suddenly and stands me up. I gasp as he kisses my neck while grabbing my breasts tightly. *Oh, God! Yes!*

I'm loving every moment of this. He's so confident, controlling, and gorgeous. He licks his way up from my neck to my jaw before his mouth ravishes my lips in a deep kiss. Out of nowhere, he slaps my breasts, making my skin tingle.

"And for your final test … let's find out if you can take my cock," he groans.

He moves toward the desk chair and sits back. He grabs my hips and pulls me to his lap with my knees on both sides of the black leather chair. His hands are digging into my skin, and I feel his cock at my entrance, teasing my pussy as he grabs my hair again.

"So fucking gorgeous," he says and thrusts himself deep inside me.

I gasp and cry out loud as I feel my insides tingle. He spreads me, filling me with every deep thrust and hard slap to my ass. Pleasure and pain mix in my mind, and, for a moment, I'm not sure where I am.

Alec begins to fuck me harder, holding tight onto my hair. "Go ahead and ride that cock, Viv," he roars.

I buck against him, using the handle of the chair for support. I slam my ass back down on his cock, taking every inch of him. He slaps my ass so hard that it echoes throughout the room. The smacking of our skin and our deep heavy breaths and moans fill the room.

"Such a filthy girl, taking another man's cock. Bet your husband is missing out on a lot. You are loving it, aren't you?"

"Yes!" I throw my head back in ecstasy.

He pulls my face down, looking into my eyes. "Look into my eyes when you fucking answer me."

"Yes! I love it so much," I moan, staring into his eyes, feeling so exposed, so aroused.

"Fuck. You feel so good, baby. So good. I'm going to come inside this pussy," he grunts and thrusts harder than he ever has before.

I can feel my entire body tightening as my eyes roll back. He is bringing this ultimate pleasure that I never felt before and never even knew existed. And I fucking love it so much, I don't want it to end.

"Come for me, baby. Come with me."

I'm lost in pleasure and losing my mind as he fucks me deeper and harder. Moans escape my lips, and I grip his shoulder. He pulls me into his arms tightly as I continue moaning against his neck.

"Let go, Viv. I'm here to catch you. Come now."

The orgasm rips through me like a hurricane. It's unreal as my pussy clenches like a vise on his dick. My whole body tenses and twitches as pleasure takes over me. Even Alec follows my lead, coming inside me with one last thrust. He groans, and I feel him spasm inside me.

My body finally gives in as I have no strength left in me. I'm completely wrecked. Not even a single muscle is willing to move in my body. I just sit there on Alec's lap with my head against his shoulder while he catches his breath, running his hand along my back, soothing me, calming me.

I don't how much time passes by, but I don't move an inch. Though this time, tiredness isn't the reason. I don't want this moment to end. I'm fearful if I move, he will get up and leave me. Luckily, he doesn't say anything, but maybe he is waiting for me to get up. *What do I do? What do I say to change his mind about us?*

I know I broke our relationship off, but knowing he would accept this part of me makes me feel guilty for ending things between us. *Please stay. Don't leave me, Alec,* I plead silently.

He sighs. "Viv, at some point, you have to get up," he whispers against my hair.

I tighten my arms around his neck. "I don't want to leave …"

"I was just here to make you feel safe for your first experience. I didn't want you to remember this as a dreadful memory. But now that you know what you want and feel more confident, you can go ahead and try this with others."

"But I don't want this to try with anyone else. I want to keep doing this with *you*."

"Why? We broke up, remember?" he says, using my words against me.

I can feel the pain scorching though my heart. He is leaving me. He doesn't want to stay. *No. No. This can't happen.*

Before I'm even aware, the tears start running down my cheeks. "I … I didn't want you to see this part of me," I mutter in a broken voice.

Suddenly, his body tenses, and he pulls me back. His brows furrow in confusion as he looks at me with soft eyes. "What do you mean?"

I look down, feeling guilt and shame engulfing me. "You were always so gentle with me … I wanted to try this lifestyle with you, but I was so scared. I was scared you would feel disgusted seeing me like this. I was scared that you would call me a freak for liking such rough stuff."

And there it is. My deepest and darkest truth that I kept buried deep down in my heart.

"You said you wanted to break up because you didn't love me anymore," he says, cupping my face.

But I still don't meet his eyes. "I tried so much to change my thoughts about this lifestyle, but every time I tried, I felt as if I was incomplete. As if I was missing something. I lied because I loved you so much and didn't want you to have to be in a relationship with a freak."

More tears run down, but this time he wipes them away with the pad of his thumb. "Viv, look at me," he says in a calm and soft voice.

When I do look at him, I see something change. Something different.

"I have been thinking about this lifestyle too. I wanted to try this new experience with you, but I didn't want to scare you away. Not everyone accepts all this," he says.

My breath catches from hearing this truth. *Why didn't he tell me before?*

"Just like you, I didn't want you to think of me as a freak, because I loved you so much. I still love you," he whispers and leans in, kissing me softly.

All this time … all this distance … this separation. We could have skipped all of that if we were only honest with each other.

"Now what?" I ask against his lips.

"Now we get out of this place, go back to my apartment, and make up for all the time we have lost by fucking."

I giggle through my tears.

"And from now on, we will be honest with each other. Also, if you want, we can explore more of our fantasies anywhere you want."

"Sounds good to me," I say.

"Well then, let's schedule our next appointment."

I giggle through my tears before wiping them away with the back of my hand. "You still love me?"

"I will always love you, Vivian. Do you love me?"

I nod, wiping away the tears and giving him a gentle smile.

He gifts me with a dark smile and grabs my jaw. "Answer when I ask you a question," he demands in his dominant dark voice.

"Yes, Doctor," I grin back, knowing the promise his voice holds for all the things he will do to me. And I'm ready to do everything with him.

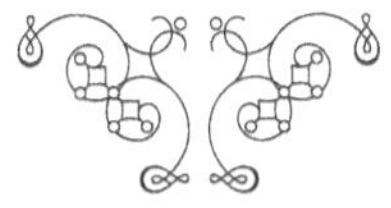

The Doll House

E. W. Farnsworth

"Hey, Barb, come out of your game-girl trance and tell me what you want to do tonight."

The svelte gamer put down her console and shook her head so that her glossy, brown hair flew in all directions. She stretched her arms and made a cat-like sound. Hearing her call, Barb's Siamese cat, Whiskers, came out of her window seat to be petted.

"I have no idea, Gloria. Why don't you choose and surprise me?"

Gloria, the blonde bombshell, looked up from her *Times* and said, "I found two new clubs we could try—The Doll House advertises an evening start with a midnight close; the other, Girls' Night, opens at one o'clock and continues until dawn. On the web, I discovered that The Doll House is exclusively lesbian with Cabaret-style naughty shows."

"Hold it right there. What's the cover?"

"There's a two-hundred-dollar cover, which includes five drinks and a private room. The sky's the limit on adds and extras. Guests can start an account or bring cash for anonymity." She raised her eyebrows inquisitively.

"So between us, we're looking at four hundred dollars just to start."

"Don't worry about the cover. I'm buying for a celebration. I just received an advance on my new romance novel. I plan to use tonight's experience in the opening chapter."

"What do you think we should do to prepare?"

"I'd planned for us to visit the sauna first. Then, we can have our mani-pedis done at Rachel's. If we plan for a light, salad lunch and skip dinner, we'll be ravenously hungry by the time the curtain goes up—and ready for anything."

"Curtain? Did you say *curtain*?"

"I did. The picture in the ad shows a tiny, curtained stage with a maniacal figure holding a whip and drawing back a curtain, behind which two nude ladies are cavorting with each other."

"Hmm. Let's see the ad."

Gloria clicked on her favorites and turned her laptop toward her roommate, who licked her lips in anticipation.

"The look of the impresario is positively diabolical. I thought you said this place was exclusively lesbian."

"It is totally lez. The person looking like a man is actually butch with a paste-on mustache. Judging by her set eyes and angular jaw, I'll bet she is one hard taskmistress. My bare bottom tingles just thinking about that whip flicking."

Barb changed her position on the couch slightly at the thought of the whip. "I'm sold. How soon can you be ready to rock?"

"Ten minutes. If we both make the bed, we cut that down to five minutes."

"I'll arrange for our ride. Since you're paying the cover, I'll pay for our ride."

The two women were out of their apartment complex in seven minutes, but the ride to the Au Naturel Sauna took another twenty. Soon, they were naked in one of the private enclosures, the steam opening their pores and driving sweat—and electrolytes—from their systems. They were relaxed when they began a cycle of showers, saunas, and glasses of fresh-squeezed orange juice, followed by dips in deep wells of waters of various temperatures. After a final shower and blow-dry, they were ready to make their transition to lunch at the Paisan Restaurant, followed by a nail treatment at Rachel's Nail Salon.

Feeling refreshed and anticipating their nail treatments, they ordered chocolate martinis with shortbread. Rachel and her all-female staff pampered the couple while they watched the film *Saturday Night Fever.*

Barb said, "I can't imagine the action of that movie taking place in the year 2020. Everything is so different now."

"Barb, that film was made in 1977! Of course, after more than four decades, the whole world has changed. For one thing, the world of sex is more than just men and women."

"Thank God for that! The Doll House would be totally illegal if the laws did not change. Still, some things are illegal."

Gloria smiled sadly. "Right you are—and for good reason. Sadism, murder, and rape are evil and ugly. From the customer reviews done on our destination, the guests and staff are clean and courteous."

Rachel overheard this exchange. "Are you ladies talking about The Doll House?"

Gloria said, "We are. Do you know the establishment?"

"I not only know it. I recommend it heartily. The shows are funny and racy with lots of audience participation. And privacy is assured, especially through the private rooms."

"Private rooms?"

"Just ask for whatever you fancy, and a stewardess will escort you to the appropriate private room. If you like sex toys, you'll go to a room full of all kinds of kinky toys. If you want to do group sex, *voila*! And if you want to explore your erogenous boundaries, masseuses are ready to give you a mink massage or a full-body shave."

"*Ooh*. That sounds divine!" said Barb.

Rachel smiled and fetched the young women another round of chocolate martinis—doubles this time, on the house. "At the door of The Doll House, just say I sent you. You'll get the best of everything. And if you don't, just let me know at your next visit here."

Gloria smiled at Barb. "The Doll House seems like a good bet." She sipped her martini and sank into her leatherette chair.

The nail techs doing her fingers and toes kept busy. The movie lumbered to its predictable conclusion.

"I'm not sure I like the male dancer ditching one girl for another."

"What do you care about those male swine? Tonight, no men are allowed." Gloria was a militant feminist, a man-hater with no mercy. She became jealous when Barb showed sympathy for the enemy. On many occasions, butch Gloria had warned her partner that any trespasses over the line of demarcation between them and men would terminate their relationship.

"Take it easy, Gloria. I must admit your eyes seem to flash fire sometimes. It makes you even more beautiful than usual."

This mollification made Gloria take a deep breath and settle back. In fact, she fell asleep and only awakened to Rachel's gentle nudging.

"Miss Swanson, I'm sorry, but it's time. I have other patrons scheduled. Take five minutes to collect yourself. Miss Hargrove is already in the lobby reading a magazine. Your ride is waiting by the curb."

"Thank you, Rachel. It won't take me a minute." She bustled to pull herself together. Checking out was easy, as Barb had paid for both of them, including the traditional large tip for the service.

"I'm feeling famished, Gloria. My stomach is growling."

"Perfect! The hungrier we are, the better the evening's play."

"Do you want to return to our apartment for a quick nap?"

"Definitely not. By the time we reach our destination uptown, it will be evening. From the descriptions I've read, entering The Doll House is like going into a perpetual night. The action is continuous, at least, until midnight."

Their driver raised her brow when the women climbed into the rear of her vehicle. "The Doll House, right?"

"That's right," Gloria said. She shook her boy-cut hair, pleased that the driver seemed to enjoy her view through the rearview mirror.

Barb was used to her partner being admired. Gloria was still a knock-out model—with a face, figure, and personality that helped her sell her romances. Barb's fingers itched to get back to her game console. Being with her friend was her second-favorite pastime. Gloria reached over and pulled her in for a lingering kiss.

"I love you, girl. Now, don't you forget that."

"I love you too, Gloria."

"Then cheer up. Maybe you can get some ideas for your new game tonight."

"You are the focus of my new game. And you know it. If I get any ideas, we can work them out together. I just like to be with you."

The driver whistled softly as she watched the lovebirds play in her back seat. Gloria thought she was whistling, "The Loneliness of Autumn," but she could not be sure.

Twenty minutes later, the vehicle pulled up in front of a nineteenth-century mansion not far from Columbia University. The brass plaque with the words "The Doll House" was the only signage. The young women liked the subtlety. The driver said she would return at midnight to "rescue" the two. All of them laughed at this idea. The car drove away as Gloria and Barb stepped arm in arm to the door and applied the brass knocker.

The interior of The Doll House featured a vestibule with a counter and coatroom. Gloria counted out four Franklins for the covers. The attendant stamped the backs of their hands with a fluorescent stamp and waved them down the hall. At the end of the hall, two giant, beautiful, scantily-clad stewardesses stood on either side of an immense door.

One asked, "What is your pleasure—the stage, or a private room?"

Gloria said, "Both, but first the stage. Check on us periodically about transitioning to a private room, please."

The stewardess gave Gloria a menu card with the choices for private rooms. She scanned the list, which was illuminated by the stewardess's penlight. Then, they were escorted through the door into the theater room. They were seated at the small table right next to the stage where a curtain was drawn, and a single wooden chair stood where the curtain closed. The stewardess disappeared into the darkness but soon reappeared with the first of the guests' drinks.

"I don't know how she manages to find people in the dark," Barb said.

"*Shh*. The show is about to begin. Here's to a great evening!" Gloria touched her glass to her friend's as the impresario stepped through the curtain with her whip snapping and the spotlight finding her satirical grin.

As the curtain pulled apart, the spotlight discovered two naked women writhing and kissing while the lead woman sang and snapped her whip. Canned music underscored the satirical lyrics. The two pink women caressed each other for a long while. Then, their spotlight went out, and the impresario stepped forward and put her foot upon the chair so everyone could see she wore no panties. She held a wireless mic and welcomed the customers in a dozen languages. She then said, in English, that she was the rule maker and that what she said went. She looked around the audience and called Barb forward.

The gamer girl stood and stepped onto the stage. She was asked to sit in the chair. To the sound of the whip snapping, she was compelled to answer questions, some factual and some embarrassing.

"Answer truly, or taste my whip." The impresario snapped the whip. "Answer untruthfully, and you will taste my whip." She repeated the snapping motion. This time, she held the end of the whip and licked it suggestively. "I love this whip. Can't you see?" The audience laughed uneasily.

She walked around the chair with Barb in it, snapping her whip. "I'll show you what this whip is really for. Go back to your seat, dear." The spotlight shone on Barb's seat beside Gloria's. Barb returned to her chair, glad she had not tasted the whip. Gloria took her hand, but she withdrew it, shaking her head. When the spotlight went out, Barb found Gloria's hand and held it.

Meanwhile, the two naked women came out in scant maids' costumes with feather dusters. They dusted the chair that Barb had sat on. The impresario snapped her whip, so the two maids stood back. With her white-gloved hand, the woman with the whip inspected the chair but found it dusty. She snapped her whip and pointed to the maid on the right, who scuttled forward and bent over the chair for her punishment. The whip came down three times, and the maid's bare bottom was streaked with three red marks. The maid curtsied and went back to her place.

"That is what my whip is for. Now we will play games." The woman laid down her whip and did a striptease act, laying her garments on the chair until she was completely naked. She paraded up and down before the audience, fondling her own breasts and turning to pull her cheeks apart at the audience. "You see, I have nothing to hide. Nothing." Slowly, she put her clothing back on. When she had finished doing that, she pointed to the maid on the left and gestured toward the chair.

The maid stepped forward and curtsied. She then stripped while dancing and ended with a flourish, but she was still wearing her high heels. As punishment for her omission, the whip came down on her bare buttocks three times, leaving its marks. The woman then pulled off her high heels and did gymnastics with the chair as her partner. The whip snapped, and she put her clothing on again seductively. She took her place next to the other maid to wait for instructions.

Finally, the three performers formed a line and sang, "Three Little Maids Are We." That ended their routine. The curtain was closed by the woman with the whip. Dim lights came up in the house. A second round of drinks came for Barb and Gloria, who spoke in low tones about the action thus far.

"Subtle it is not," Gloria said. "I'm certainly glad that witch did not beat your bare bottom. Her whip makes wicked marks, doesn't it?"

"I can only imagine being one of those maids, beaten every night to make their living. They are beautiful—and they must work out often and eat little to keep their figures."

A voice behind them screeched, "Of course, they are professionals. They do what they must to survive." The sound of a whip snapping identified the owner of the voice.

"I don't suppose you know how your whip feels?"

"We shall see. Why don't you come backstage with me now? If your friend doesn't mind, you can become part of the show."

Barb nodded with a smile. Gloria stood and accepted the impresario's hand as her guide. She disappeared through the curtain and went backstage. A stewardess brought Barb another drink and sat with her own drink in Gloria's chair. The dim lights became dimmer until they faded completely. Barb sat in darkness for two minutes. Then, the curtains parted to reveal the bare bottom of the impresario, who had bent over to receive a whipping administered by Gloria, who was dressed like a male lumberjack.

"Please don't beat me again," the woman with the mustache pleaded.

Gloria snapped the whip and said, "Be silent and take your punishment."

The woman with the pink bottom danced from foot to foot, anticipating her whipping. Gloria's eyes glistened as she warmed to her task. Her hand fell once, twice, three times. The red marks showed the whip had struck home.

The woman gingerly stepped back and turned to face the audience. "Is there anyone else here who thinks she deserves to be punished? Come now, don't be shy. We have all done horrible things to each other. We all need to be beaten without mercy. You don't believe me? Where are my little maids?"

The two maids appeared again with their dusters. In pantomime, the stage mistress wagged her finger in each maid's face. Then, she took the whip out of Gloria's hands and gestured for the maids to bend over and show their bare buttocks. She beat the women's behinds with three strokes each.

Then, she gestured for them to stand back. She gave Gloria a choice: "You may return to your seat, or have your seat warmed with my whip. Which do you choose?"

Gloria walked backward to the little table where the stewardess rose to relinquish her chair. Gloria sat, still wearing her lumberjack costume, while the players on stage sang songs to piped music. When the lights faded and the curtain closed, a few minutes of darkness were followed by the rise of dim lights. The stewardess, who had remained by their table, asked them whether they needed another drink.

"No, thank you, stewardess, but my friend and I would like to try number three on your private room menu."

"That is an excellent choice. Please bring your drinks and follow me."

The stewardess led Gloria and Barb behind the little stage and down a narrow hallway to a door marked with the number three. The stewardess opened the door and said, "We shall be right with you. In the meantime, you may take off your clothes, lie on the bed and play with the toys if you like."

Gloria and Barb put their drinks down on the side tables and took off all their clothing. While Gloria flopped on the bed and examined herself in the ceiling mirror, Barb explored the toys in the huge toy boxes that lined the walls. She handled the toys one by one. She particularly liked a unique, leather device that appeared to be a curved stick with a leather dildo on each end.

"Look what I've found!" she said. As she fondled the device, it began to vibrate automatically. It seemed to be alive the way it swelled and shrunk in cycles. The young women wondered how this marvelous device could be used to mutual advantage. Suddenly, the door was flung open, and the two giant stewardesses entered, completely nude.

One of the stewardesses said, "I see you've found the double dildo. We'll show you how to use this toy. Give it to me, please. And pass the pot of lubricating gel."

Barb did as she was told while the second stewardess lay down beside Gloria in the bed.

"You don't want to be harmed as the dildo slides into you. Use plenty of gel on the outside of the dildo and along your labia. Naomi will show you how it's done."

The giantess on the bed slathered one side of the dildo with goo, and she applied an equal amount to her labia. She grasped the dildo by the opposite end and inserted it into her vagina. She moaned as the instrument plumbed her depths.

"What about the other end of the dildo?" Gloria asked.

"Watch me," the other stewardess said.

She applied the gel to the upright portion of the dildo until it was covered on all sides. She then used her index finger to spread the gel over her labia. "Watch carefully. As

I sit down while spreading myself with my hands, the toy will begin to vibrate slowly. When the toy swells inside me, it shrinks and withdraws in my partner's vagina."

"Be careful, Beth. Do you want me to sit up a bit?"

"I should be okay at this angle, Naomi." She eased the free end of the dildo into her vagina. The double dildo began to vibrate.

Naomi grasped the pillow behind her head and closed her eyes.

Beth lowered herself until she could go no lower. She seemed to rock in ecstasy as the toy did its work. "I don't want us to have all the fun. Why don't you two find another double dildo and do as we just did?"

Barb did not have to be asked twice. She rummaged through the toys until she found another double dildo. She was clearly anticipating delight as she applied the goo and inserted the device into the cleft below her partner's belly. She saw how Gloria was bucking from joy. Quickly, she applied the gel to the other end of the dildo, and, not forgetting to slather her genitals, she sat on the dildo, drawing its full length into her vagina. She moaned as the vibrations started. Gloria moaned as well. The instrument laved them both in alternating, juddering strokes. Barb felt her end of the dildo touch her inmost core. In the cycle, Gloria felt her cervix caressed softly by the dildo just when it was time for the toy to retract to please her partner.

For a while, the four young women enjoyed their toys. Barb was convinced that she and Gloria should buy a double dildo right away. Naomi announced she was having an orgasm. Not to be outdone, Gloria said the same.

Beth looked at Barb. "They are having orgasms because they are on the bottom. If they were on the top as we are, they would be a little slower getting there."

Barb struggled against the dildo. She squeezed hard around the solid, thick, imitation penis. She was gasping slightly, and her eyes blinked.

Noticing her condition, Beth said, "Don't force it. Just go with the rhythm. Breathe regularly. Keep undulating with the toy. Believe me, the joy will be worth it."

Barb followed the stewardess's instructions. She felt her insides trembling. Her mind seemed to flood with good feelings. "I'm coming. I feel as if my insides are going to explode. *Ngh. Aah.* I can't believe that feeling."

Beth said, "I feel the same way. I'm finally coming. Now I'm going to wait until my partner Naomi feels it too."

Naomi was almost delirious with joy. She was shuddering and trembling in concert with her partner. "*Ooh.* I can't believe it. I've never felt it this strong before."

Four women, four orgasms, each reinforcing the others.

When the women fell apart on the bed, Gloria said, "I've never experienced anything like it. Whew. I want to do it all over again."

The others needed to rest for a moment. That's when the door swung open to reveal the impresario.

"Did you say that you wanted to experience the double dildo again? Stay where you are. I'll oblige you."

She found a third double dildo in the toy box and brought it for Gloria to see. She anointed one end with gel and used her gooey finger to cover the genitals of her customer. Her finger found Gloria's clitoris and worked it gently until the young woman cried out for the insertion. So the impresario inserted the gooey end of the dildo into the woman and heard her cry in delight. She then put gel on the other end of the toy and on her own labia. She rose and inserted the toy into her vagina. As she lowered herself, the toy slid deep inside her.

Her eyes fluttered, and she moaned in delight. "I have to be back on stage soon, but I don't want this to stop—ever."

The motion of the machine began laving inside both women. They moaned in alternation.

Gloria was the first to experience an orgasm. "I don't believe I'm having another orgasm." She was bucking upward to receive the dildo against her core. She used her vagina to squeeze the device, and her orgasm's intensity increased. She bucked and screamed in delight.

The figure above her smiled maliciously. "I'll have to spank your bare bottom, you naughty child."

Gloria used her fists to pound on the chest of her tormenter. She groaned and pressed upward. She was frantic to attain heights of joy that she had never experienced. Barb was jealous to hear her lover's cries when she was not the partner giving Gloria such pleasure.

The two stewardesses saw Barb's anguish, and they moved swiftly to provide a remedy. They quickly applied goo to two dildos, which they applied front and back to Barb and to themselves. Barb was not accustomed to having two partners, but she surrendered to the new experience, enjoying one woman in the front and another in the back simultaneously.

Not long afterward, Barb was oblivious to what was happening to her. She only knew she had never had sex like this in her entire life. Two Nubian giantesses and two electronic toys were taking her to the limit. She was somewhat afraid of what was happening, but the stewardesses seemed to know what they were doing.

So, Barb had one orgasm after another. She said, "*Ngh.*" She said, "*Ooh.*" She wanted to stop, but the women urged her to give them gratification too.

Soon, all three women were conjoined in ecstasy. Gloria heard their moans and groans, and those nearly drove her out of her mind. So, five-a-bed, the young women enjoyed each other. They strained and became exhilarated. They achieved frequent orgasms. They sweat and tangled the sheets. When they all broke apart, panting and gasping, they knew they had found what they had been looking for.

The first to leave the room was the impresario, who was a little late to answer her cue. The stewardesses were next. They looked at each other as if to say, "Where else could we work where we had better results?"

Finally, Gloria and Barb lay smelling the female scents that suggested satisfaction. There was no hint of testosterone or musk in the air. No threats of conception struck fear in their hearts. They had hit the moon, experienced rain and clouds, and felt their way toward Nirvana, all without males.

"Do you feel okay, Barb?"

"I've never felt better! And how are you doing?"

"Just great. I'm not sure I'll be able to stand for a while. I hope this place has showers."

As if on command, the stewardesses reentered the room to show the young women to an adjoining, spacious bathroom with big, fluffy towels and bathrobes. Gloria prepared their bath, and Barb slid into the sudsy water alongside her partner.

When the stewardesses had retreated, Gloria said, "I don't think I've ever been more gratified in my life."

Barb said, "Likewise. I don't think men have a clue about how to satisfy a woman."

"I agree. Now we have a difficult choice: we can depart with the memories we have created together, or we can go to the next level by ordering up another private room."

"I'll think about that. On the one hand, we are in a place that changes perspectives. On the other hand, we don't want to become disappointed by an experience that has thus far been optimal."

The bathroom door opened, and the impresario was followed by the two maids, each carrying a tray with the ladies' fourth drinks.

She said, "Here are the fourth of your five drinks. Let me suggest that you return to the theater room to see more shows. Then, you can book another private room if you like. The house is filling up fast at this hour. Decide at your leisure. The choice is entirely yours." She kissed the two women on the mouth, but she spent a long time using her tongue on Gloria's lips and mouth.

Barb had misgivings about staying later, but Gloria, energized by kisses, thought they should at least finish the drinks they had paid for.

The two young women rose from their bubble bath and dried off. Gloria discovered that her own clothes had been returned in exchange for the lumberjack costume she had earlier worn on stage. Barb slipped into her evening costume, ready to begin anew.

Naomi, the lead stewardess, escorted them to their small table near the stage. She conveyed their fourth drinks from room number three to the stage table. She retreated, but not far enough to be challenged to satisfy her two guests' every whim.

The impresario interrupted her song to introduce Gloria and Barb, but not by name. The spotlight caught the two women kissing and touching their glasses together.

It was clear from their smiles that they were having a night full of happiness in a cold, ruthless city.

The mistress of ceremonies went through her repertoire of beating the bare buttocks of her maids and threatening to do the same to recalcitrant members of her audience, who laughed or screamed in delight in equal measure.

When she beckoned to Barb to come to the stage for her punishment, Barb played along like a good sport. The two Nubian giantesses seized her, pulled up her dress, and pulled down her panties. The whip came down three times in swift succession. The stewardesses pulled up the young woman's panties again around her bottom, which bore the tell-tale red marks. Barb then stood at the back of the stage while Gloria was subjected to the same fate as she.

Gloria was surprised to find herself looking at the floor while her dress was pulled up, and her panties were pulled down. She felt the hot sting of the whip falling on her bare bottom three times. Hot tears of indignation streamed down her face. Then, she found herself standing next to her partner as the music came up and the lights went down on the evening's show.

But the show was not entirely over yet. Gloria and Barb were served their fifth and final drink at their little table by the stage. The other customers departed, laughing and fondling each other. Some looked with sympathy toward the two women who had borne the brunt of the finale. A photographer snapped a picture of the two women, and that was the signal for the lights to come fully on.

The impresario came to their table to bid them *adieu*.

"That was a dirty trick you played on us," Gloria told the woman.

"It was a better trick than any man would have turned. With them, you would have felt defiled and might possibly have become pregnant. Here, you had pleasure as you never experienced before, with none of the drawbacks. Admit it! And you'll leave with a memory you'll never forget. If you have any misgivings, you know you have already been punished for what you have done. The whip on your bare buttocks—can anything be clearer? So, as you go home to reflect on your experience, think deeply if you will ever experience a better microcosm of life. If you think this was a worthwhile evening, come again. If not, take your lessons into account as you re-enter your quotidian routines."

The two women found their ride outside the building. All smiles, the driver was anxious to know how their evening went.

Gloria spoke for both women when she said, "The evening had its ups and downs. The ups were great. As for the downs, we'll see. I'm having difficulty sitting properly now. Go easy on the bumps." She reached for Barb's hand and found it.

The two women held to each other as they wound through the sad and empty city streets to their apartment. They later agreed that they had experienced a night to remember.

They found a sex toy shop that sold them double dildos and a gel like the one that had been applied at The Doll House. They tried the devices on many occasions, but the results were not uniform—and nothing like the first time. As their memories of that fatal night faded, they kept one thing in mind: the whip landing on their bare bottoms and the lingering sting of penance for joys they would never experience in any other way.

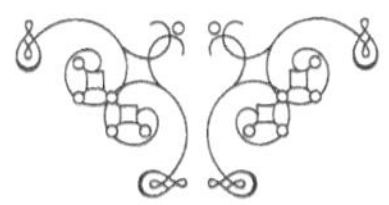

The Fantasy Club

Wolfgang Domino

The sun rose in beautiful pink streaks. It was a good sign because Christina planned on going on horseback for a few hours. The walk down to the barn was nice as she listened to the cicadas click in the trees. She smiled at the morning dew changing the color of her boots. The beautiful, fragrant scent of spring encapsulated her. The country always felt like home. Christina couldn't imagine herself living in the city, or anywhere but on a farm.

"Good morning, Star," she whispered, reaching through the hardwood fence to touch the massive horse's muzzle. The fur was soft.

Christina opened the gate, pulled the horse out by its guide, and stopped in the center of the barn. It was a big, beautiful animal with white and brown hair. She set down a bucket of oats on the floor and began gathering her riding gear. This was their ritual on weekends. Her father, who was a hard ass, would let her roam on Saturday mornings.

Their last conversation rang through her mind from the night before: "You steer clear of that Dyer girl. She isn't any good. She's loose." That was a typical witticism from her father. If they weren't loose, they were tramps. He had a name for everyone in town who didn't work on their farm. Even if they did, sometimes he gave them nicknames too.

Mandy Dyer had been Christina's best friend for the first couple of years of high school. It was more of convenience than compatibility. She lived on the farm closest to the Pearson's, and her daddy's assessment of Mandy wasn't wrong. Mandy had given her virginity away before freshman year. All the boys in high school wanted to be her friend for obvious reasons. Now that they'd both graduated, the attention had gone down some, but the rumors still swarmed the town when the boys got together.

According to the rumors, Mandy had been on the receiving end of every sexual situation imaginable. One boy said he'd had a threesome with her and another girl. Another guy said he and a couple of others tag-teamed her at a party once. If there were a sex story in the sleepy little town, you'd bet Mandy Dyer was at the bottom of it.

Star was crunching at the bucket of oats while Christina was working the saddle onto her back. Christina, who was a hardworking country girl, looked forward to the opportunity to get away from her father. Several times she thought about moving out, but she didn't think it was a good idea yet. Her father still needed her. The farm had come on to some tough times. Even though she was an adult, her father felt the need to treat her like a child sometimes. He was overprotective and cautious of who she hung around.

When Star finished breakfast, Christina kicked the bucket out of the way, climbed on her back, and stormed out of the building. They sauntered for a bit, just taking it easy until they got to the path. When they reached the path, Christina tapped on the reigns, letting Star gallop faster. The wind blew through her black hair, blowing it into streams behind her. While they were moving,

Christina felt free. All of her responsibilities seemed to melt.

Trees blew past her as they trotted through the woods. It wasn't uncommon to share the path with fellow riders, but it was rare for them to be out this early in the morning. Christina and Star had gone nearly a mile when Christina was surprised to hear another horse galloping nearby. It was a small town, and she was almost guaranteed to know whoever was riding out there with her. It was also a friendly town, so she didn't feel afraid to call out to her neighbor.

"Hello?" she called into the woods. "It's Christina," she added.

"Chris. How the hell are you?" a female voice returned.

The voice belonged to Mandy Dyer. The galloping got closer, and before Christina knew it, Dyer and her horse, Buttercup, stopped beside them.

Even if the rumors were true about Mandy being a slut, she was beautiful. If she didn't live in a Podunk town, she'd probably have a modeling job somewhere in the big city. It wasn't a surprise all the boys in town loved her. She had huge tits and a rocking body. She also had a calm, welcoming face, which you couldn't help but like at first glance. One of her most prominent features was her big, kissable lips.

"It's been a long time, Mandy. How have you been?" Christina was genuinely glad to see her, even against her father's warnings.

"Good!" she said, climbing off the horse.

It was clear Mandy wanted to talk, so Christina climbed off her horse as well, and they both tied them to nearby trees. Buttercup and Star found some shrubbery to enjoy while the ladies caught up.

"I never see you anymore," Mandy said, grabbing Christina in a big hug. Her huge breasts pushed against Christina's average ones.

"I know. I have been busy."

"We have to hang out sometime. I go into the city all the time. There are some of the coolest clubs. They have just about anything that might suit your fancy."

There was something about Mandy's smile that was implying something, but Christina wasn't sure what it was.

"It's fun," Mandy added.

It wasn't abundantly clear what she meant by that, but it seemed interesting.

Mandy's straight, brown hair clung to her back. The girls wore identical riding gear, but Mandy filled it out better. She had beautiful eyes, which seemed to glisten in the morning sun. Mandy was also one of those girls who figured out how to do their makeup flawlessly from an early age.

"I don't get out much," Christina admitted. Aside from her twenty-first birthday, she'd never set foot in a bar. Even then, it was with her older brother, Clyde. They hadn't painted the town or anything. They'd gone out, had a single beer, and gone home.

"Do you have a boyfriend now?" Mandy asked.

"No. After Jeremy and I broke up, I haven't dated since."

"You have to get back out there, girl. You're missing out."

Again, Christina didn't know what she was referring to, but she was curious. "Missing out on what?"

"Sex, of course. You have done it before, right?" Mandy asked, looking her over.

At this, Christina turned bright pink. "Yes. Jeremy was my first and my only so far."

Mandy gave her a sideways glance and added a scoff for good measure. "See. I told you, missing out. I'm not going to give you a number or anything. Don't slut-shame me either," she giggled.

The town rumors had been true, not that Christina spent much time doubting them. Her brother Clyde had a lot of friends who came by the farm, and they would talk. Sometimes, they would talk about the local girls, leaving the subject of Mandy open often. While feeding the pigs or the chickens, Christina had overheard some of the things she'd done with the local men. It hadn't been appalling, those stories she heard.

Christina hadn't been prepared to have this conversation. The relationship with Mandy had faded a long time ago, and she didn't know if she felt comfortable talking about sex with her former best friend. Christina couldn't fight the red streaks crossing her face. "I don't know," Christina said, dragging her feet through the dirt.

"Listen. The type of club I am talking about is completely cool. You don't have to do anything you don't want to." The calmness in her voice was comforting.

"What kind of club are you talking about?" Christina asked.

There was a pause as if Mandy was considering how to respond with dignity and grace. "It's a club for hooking up. It is entirely about completing fantasies." Mandy clapped a hand on Christina's shoulder. "I understand you're shy, but I promise it's worth the experience. You can choose from many different rooms, and in each room is a specific fantasy: BDSM, anal, foot fetish, group sex."

The word *anal* dropped like a brick. Christina knew what it was, heard about people doing it, but had never been curious enough to dig. Even now, thinking about a room entirely devoted to that sexual act, she thought she'd pass.

Christina tried to cut the conversation short, telling herself she wouldn't go to such a place. After all, she was too shy. Christina, who had grown up a devout Christian, who had gone to church every Sunday since she could remember, didn't think she could be in a place like that. The idea of being in a room while people were having sex seemed odd—not to mention her getting involved. She thought about sex in a reserved way. It was for one couple, behind closed doors.

"I found out about this place from the back of a men's magazine," Mandy continued. "My ex Greg had them lying around his apartment. One day, I was bored and flipped through one. It turned out there was a club near us, and I thought about it every day until Greg and I broke up."

Mandy unhinged her horse, climbed on its back, and looked at her. "Promise you will think about it in a nonjudgmental way," Mandy said before galloping off.

I don't think I could ever do something like that, Christina thought. *I'd be so embarrassed.* Christina tried to imagine what it would be like inside the fantasy club. Every time she tried to imagine it, she couldn't even put herself in the room.

Later that night, Christina couldn't stop thinking about the club. It was too bizarre not to consider the things she said about going and fulfilling her fantasies. When everyone in the house was asleep, Christina went on the website and looked at the information. Mandy had been right. The place was designed to focus on major fetishes. According to the site, there was more than one Fantasy Fulfillment Club, and there were a couple of camps as well. The company prided itself on how clean and safe they were.

I don't think I have any fetishes, Christina thought. *I don't think I have any kinks either.* From her relationship with Jeremy, she tried to remember specifics about their sex life. The more she thought about it, the more it seemed vanilla. As she was scrolling through the descriptions of the rooms, there was one that intrigued her. If she were going to go to the club, there was one room she thought she'd enter: a room in the back referred to as the "Glory Hole Room."

Strangers would stick their cocks through a hole in the wall, and whatever happened, happened. The site provided videos. There was a man with his veiny cock sticking through the hole, and on the other side was another man sucking. Right next to that was another cock protruding from the wall, and a woman backed up against it, pounding herself against the wall.

Originally, Christina intended to look at the video once, but she couldn't stop herself from watching it a second and a third time. There was something about the anonymity that intrigued her. She could walk into this room and get laid. She didn't have to go out on a date and work her charm. There wouldn't be any awkward kiss in front of the door. It seemed so easy. The opportunity to have sex had never been so simple.

That night, while lying in bed, Christina dreamt about the fantasy club. In her dream, she walked into the BDSM room. She stopped there, watching a man and a woman both in full leather. The woman, a busty blonde, was tied up. The man lubed a plug and pushed it into her. The man, tall and covered in shimmery leather, slapped her ass with a cat-o'-nine-tails, hard. Across her ass and her upper legs were red marks.

Christina didn't feel bad for the woman. She thought it looked fun, providing they had a safe word. The man in the leather gimp suit walked around her and opened her leather vest, exposing her huge breasts. He took a couple of clamps from a wall and clipped them on to her nipples. That, she seemed to enjoy. The woman seemed to purr like a kitten, lust firing in her eyes.

When Christina woke, she had a different perspective on the fantasy club. At first, she had been judgmental. Now, she understood why people would go. Some people wanted to have sex without a relationship. They just wanted sex. Maybe they liked being single. Christina climbed off the bed to get dressed and realized she'd soaked her panties. When she was changing her clothes, she made her final decision.

A few days passed, and Christina couldn't shake the club from her mind. Now, she didn't look at it in a negative light. She looked at it curiously. At first, she didn't want to admit it to Mandy, or even to herself. Now, she thought she might take her former friend up on the opportunity. It seemed like they might have some fun there. The Glory Hole Room intrigued her, and she wanted to see it with her own eyes, not the short clip on the site.

While tending to the farm, Christina found herself slipping in and out of fantasies. All of the fantasies took place in the club. While driving the tractor, she thought about the Glory Hole Room. When she was feeding the pigs, she thought about group sex. She'd never been with more than one man. She'd never been with a woman either. The idea didn't seem a million miles away, not like it had just a week before.

While grocery shopping in town, Christina bumped into her friend Mandy in the cereal aisle. Surrounded by cardboard boxes and busy shoppers, the two women started chatting.

"I may take you up on the offer," Christina admitted. Over time, the idea had whittled its way through her thick skin.

"Oh?" Mandy looked intrigued.

"It's been a long time since Jeremy. I checked it out on the website, and it doesn't look as bad as I thought." Christina looked around, making sure there weren't any nosy people looking at them. "Do you have a favorite room?"

Mandy thought long and hard about this. "Yeah, I like the BDSM Room. There is something about being controlled that I love. Sometimes, you need someone to push you around. I go for the hardcore package that includes foxtails, hot wax, stuff like that. Honestly, I love the pain." There was a flicker in Mandy's eyes when she said that.

Christina had an exceptional imagination, and it didn't take much to put Mandy into a room with a leather-wearing man wielding a whip. It didn't seem like a stretch to imagine her tied up, half-naked, being slapped around by a man in a mask either.

"I was looking into the Glory Hole Room. It looks like it could be fun," Christina struggled to say in a mousey voice. Even when the words came from her mouth, they seemed foreign.

"Oh, it is. I think that was the first room I went into, and it took me three rounds of watching before I got into the flow."

"You were nervous too?" Christina asked.

"The truth is, people who have been doing it for a long time are nervous. Everyone is nervous, but nobody in there is trying to hurt each other. Well, unless they are in the BDSM Room," she chuckled. "It's interesting and different, but once you get into the idea, it's freeing. I haven't been on a bad date in like a year."

When the two parted from the cereal aisle, her mind was at ease. They planned to get together the following weekend. Mandy was going to pick her up and drive her to the club. They planned on going later because there were bound to be fewer people. Usually, by eleven o'clock, the majority of regular guests have gone home.

Christina was nervous about going to the club. She'd never done anything of the sort before, but she had to admit her little secret was intoxicating. The forbidden aspect played well in her mind. A couple of times, she thought about canceling, but she couldn't bring herself to pick up the phone. The bottom line was, she knew if she didn't go, she would regret it. There would always be unanswered questions.

Mandy picked her up on Saturday night. The two of them were sitting in Mandy's cramped little truck in the parking lot. Christina had to talk herself up in her head. Mandy was sitting there, sliding through her phone while Christina was internally having a crisis.

I can do this, Christina continued to tell herself. *There's nothing to it. I walk in the door, say hello to whoever speaks to me, and I sit in the back of whatever room, watching. I don't have to partake. Nobody is going to make me. Nobody is going to touch me without consent.*

The music could be heard pulsing from the parking lot. The neon sign was inviting and glowed bright green. What concerned Christina was the lack of windows, but she understood the need for privacy. A couple of people passed them on the way in, chuckling and talking about how fun it was.

It was quainter than Christina originally anticipated. There were sofas in the front room and a bar. The front room looked more like a lounge than a club, but the music was pumping from further in the building. The environment was more relaxed. People of all genders and races gathered in the front room. Some of them wore skimpy outfits, while others were fully dressed. Everyone was talking, and nobody even noticed they'd entered the room. On the first couch was a beautiful, ebony woman who was getting her neck kissed and sucked by a tall, thin man.

"Would you like a drink to calm the nerves?" Mandy asked, pointing to the bar.

"Please," Christina agreed.

Suddenly, she felt overdressed. Christina had gone with a nice-looking, but rather standard, purple blouse, and a pair of khaki pants. At first, she thought she wanted to wear a skirt, but thought better of it because she didn't want anyone with curious fingers to have easier access.

Mandy wore a plaid skirt and fishnets with incredible confidence. She looked good too. For a top, Mandy chose a white belly shirt, exposing her midriff. Christina hadn't been turned on by a female before, but Mandy looked great. It could be the night to try all sorts of new things.

The line at the bar was minimal, and Mandy returned with a fruity cocktail bearing an umbrella. Christina didn't seem to care what the drink was, or even what was in it. The second it was in her hand, she tipped it back and slugged down a mouthful. After a few minutes, she began to feel its impact. The drink was liquid courage, and some of the stress began to evaporate.

Mandy passed a man in leather shorts. They spoke for a couple of seconds, but the music was too loud to eavesdrop. The man knew her by name. Under his shirt, the man had nipple clamps or chains. Christina could see the outline of them. They spoke briefly, getting close enough to hear each other talk. The conversation was short and sweet.

"That was Charles. He wanted to know if I was going into the BDSM Room tonight. We have fun in there. He's a great dom."

A long, white hallway reached out from the lobby. The first opening to the right had beads instead of a door. Three people stood in line, looking at Christina and Mandy as they walked down the hall.

"This is the foot room," Mandy said. "You can go to display or play." Through the beads, a man could be seen sucking on a woman's toes, who was standing on a platform above him. "I have done the display before. It isn't half bad. A man sucking on your toes is better than you may think."

The second room had an actual door. Above the doorway was a simple sign labeled "BDSM."

"This is where the hot and heavy stuff goes down. I spend most of my time here. You can choose to be a sub or a dom. I always go as a sub. I tried to dominate once, and I couldn't do it. It's not for me."

Through the thick door, a whip could be heard cracking against something Christina presumed to be skin. They moved forward.

"Ah, The Hole," Mandy muttered. "If you're looking for anonymous sex, this is the place to be. If you go through the first door, you're on the giving end. If you go through the second door, you're on the receiving end."

From the door to the Glory Hole Room, they could see another room, which wasn't labeled. That room, Mandy told her, was for group sex. They weren't close enough to hear anything, but according to her friend, it got quite loud in there. She'd been inside a few times.

The Hole was the room that fascinated Christina most. It was the thing that made her want to go in the first place. There was something about the anonymity that she loved. If she wanted to get a man off, or if she wanted to practice, this was the place to do it without restraint.

"Can we peek inside?"

"Yeah, sure." Mandy pointed to the light above the door. "Green means go. Red means the room is either occupied or closed." The light was currently green.

Christina stood in front of the door, holding her hand out. A moment passed before she mustered the courage to open it. Inside was a blank room with the outline of two men drawn on one wall. It seemed rather simple. Where the outlined man's crotch would be was a hole that passed into the next room.

"It's pretty simple. You walk up there and press that red button. If a man is back there, he will come out through the hole, and you can do whatever you want. It's adventurous. During the busier hours, there is always a line here. It works the other way too, sometimes. Once in a while, there will be a girl on the other side of the wall, but not as often. In that case, the cutout in the wall changes. Pretty easy to do."

"That's, um, interesting," Christina said, trying not to come off as shy as she was. For a moment, Christina imagined herself on display, on the far side of the wall for anyone to take. There was something delicious about that thought, but she wasn't ready to explore that fantasy yet. She wanted to start small.

"Do you want to see if someone is back there?" Mandy asked, approaching the outline.

"No," Christina blurted, then immediately regretted it.

"It's all right to be nervous," Mandy said before hitting the button. "I will go first. If you feel like it, you can join in."

Without any hesitation, Mandy slapped the red button, and a bell rang on the other side of the wall. There was a pause before a door opened, and a hard cock slid through the hole.

"Well, it looks like we have a taker." Mandy laughed. She approached the stiff cock protruding from the wall, grabbed it, and began to tug. "Already nice and hard," she said, jerking him off. Mandy looked down, spit a wad of saliva onto his cock and continued to rub it up and down. There wasn't an ounce of shyness in Mandy's approach. "I like it, big boy," she muttered.

It didn't take long before Mandy was on her knees, and the anonymous cock was bobbing in and out of her mouth. She seemed to enjoy sucking it because she looked like she was having a great time. The man behind the wall must have been grateful too, as his grunts could be heard through the lulls in the music.

"Don't be shy," Mandy whispered. With a single finger, Mandy beckoned Christina to join her.

At first, she didn't want to get involved, but watching Mandy suck off this stranger had done something to her. She didn't want to admit that she was turned on, but she couldn't deny it either. Christina walked across the room and continued to watch Mandy. She was considering doing something when Mandy took her hand and placed it on the erect penis. Christina played with it a little, pulling it up and down. It felt good, hard. It was bigger than Jeremy's had been. Having her hand on the cock made her feel powerful.

"Don't be afraid," Mandy ushered her. Mandy grabbed the cock and popped it back into her mouth as if to show her that it was going to be fine. "It won't bite," she chuckled.

Christina lowered herself to her knees, approaching the cock apprehensively. It wasn't like when she slept with Jeremy. She'd known who it was then. There was trust, but she couldn't do anything with him without fear of shame. Christina pulled her hair back before enveloping the cock with her lips. She slid it in, feeling the moisture from Mandy's lips. She sucked, pulling it up and down, riding her lips across the shaft.

When Christina pulled back for air, Mandy took over. She placed the dick back in her mouth and began to suck, pulling it back and forth, using her lips like the best weapon ever invented. The two of them took turns sucking and jerking until finally, the man spit unexpectedly, cum landing on the floor between them.

"It's only polite to clean up when you finish," Mandy said. She licked the cum off the tip of his cock.

The dick withdrew through the hole and disappeared.

Christina didn't know what to think of what just happened. She had done her first double blowjob, and she wasn't sure if it was a good thing or not, but she thought the man who received must have been satisfied. Mandy looked like she had fun, and she couldn't deny that it was an interesting experience. Christina didn't feel like she wanted to flee the club; rather, she wanted to go and explore another room.

"How was that?" Mandy asked, getting up from the floor and moving for the door. They had no practical reason to stay.

"Well, it was certainly interesting. Maybe you can go into the other room, and I can watch? Do you think that could work?"

Mandy wasn't sure if that was a thing or not, but she thought it wouldn't matter. There had been a line in the hall when they walked past earlier, but there wasn't one when they arrived this time. Mandy said she never had someone else in the room before, but she didn't think the dominant would mind since Christina was new. "Nobody wants to go into something like that completely blind. Not unless they are a huge masochist."

The room wasn't very big. Whips, chains, clamps, and all sorts of materials clung to the walls. The room was intimidating for Christina, who'd never seen that much sexual hardware before. There were dildos strapped to the walls and butt plugs in a glass display case like cupcakes at a bakery. Huge tubs of lube sat on the counters. There were different sized floggers and a healthy selection of candles.

In the center of the room was a table low enough for someone to climb on with cuffs built into the edges. It was like a small dungeon. Leather and latex shimmered on the whips and cuffs. It looked like someone had come through and polished these items. Christina had never seen a full gimp suit before in her life, but one was in the room, attached to nails on a wall.

While walking into the room, Christina's jaw dropped. Mandy noticed that look. It had been the same look she'd given the first time she walked through the door. That had been a long time ago. Now, Mandy had used almost everything in the room—some things she'd used more than once. Mandy was what the locals considered a frequent flier. She was also one of the best subs. Mandy never had trouble getting a "date" from the lounge out front.

A man walked through the door shortly after they did. He wasn't wearing a black gimp suit like Christina expected. The man was semi-formal looking, dressed nicely in a button-up shirt. "Get on the table," he spoke firmly. The handsome, strong-looking man wrenched up his sleeves.

Instead of being intimidated, Mandy smiled at Christina and walked over to the table. She hopped up and then laid down on her back.

The man walked across the room to the whips and began to look through them. "Do you want to play too?" he asked Christina.

"No, thanks. I want to watch for the first time."

"Sit in the corner and keep quiet," he said. He used that dominant voice, not knowing that speaking to Christina in such a way turned her on a bit.

There was a black whip, leather with tons of tendrils. The man selected that one and pulled it down from the wall, running his fingers through the straps. "This one should work just fine," he muttered. His shoes slapped the floor as he walked around the table, looking at Mandy like a hunk of meat. "You know the safe word," he said.

"Yes," she agreed.

"Say it," he said loudly.

"Pineapple."

The man turned her over, pulling down her plaid skirt while he did so. Under it was a white thong and pale legs. The man snapped the whip, leaving a giant, red line across her backside. "That's nice," he grumbled, moving around her again. The whip flopped in his hand for a second as he adjusted to its weight.

"Again," Mandy chimed.

The anonymous man lifted his arm, stroking her backside with the leather tendrils of the whip. The sound cracked like thunder and left another red line across her rear. The man was gritting his teeth. He slapped her ass cheek with his bare hand, leaving a print.

"Yes," she whispered, clearly in a touch of pain and glory.

Again, the man returned to the wall, which reminded Christina of her father's workshop, but with giant rubber cocks hanging on nails instead of tools. There was a rope hanging. The man selected that, and he chose something else, but Christina couldn't tell what it was, as his back had been to her.

The mysterious man, tall and handsome, walked over to Mandy. He grabbed her shirt, lifted it off her body, and tossed it on the floor. He unsnapped her bra and tossed that on the floor too. Before she could get into the position he wanted, he grabbed her arm. In the hand opposite of the one holding the rope, he had a pair of nipple clamps. He opened one, led it down to her breast, and clamped the tip of her nipple.

The face Mandy made was a grimace at first, but it changed to pleasure after a couple of seconds. "Oh," she grumbled, raising her eyebrows at the man.

The man turned, looked at Christina with curiosity for a moment before snapping the clamp on the other nipple. "Is this what you were expecting?" he asked her.

"Sort of, yes."

Christina couldn't help putting herself in Mandy's shoes. The more she thought about it, the more she could feel the clamps like they were attached to her breasts. She envisioned the pain and tried to imagine what it would be like to enjoy that feeling.

The man began to tie Mandy up, winding the rope around her hands and feet. "I like my subs to feel both pain and pleasure simultaneously. I think it's the joy of having sex." The man reached over, grabbed the whip, and slapped her again, hard. His big hands disappeared into the front of her panties for a second. Mandy spread her legs, embracing the grope.

While his hand was jostling in the front of her panties, Mandy groaned. Her hips jerked and twisted, assisting him with touching the right spot. She gyrated on the table. "Yes, daddy," she said seductively.

"I almost forgot," the man said. He walked across the room, found a ball gag, and returned to Mandy. He stuffed it in her mouth. "I wouldn't want you to scare anyone in the hall," he muttered.

The mysterious man didn't know that Mandy was a professional. She wasn't going to tell him either. She was going to be a good sub and let him do whatever he wanted, even if she'd done it all before. The man cracked the whip again before discarding it on the floor. He reached over, grabbed her skirt, and pulled it all the way off. His hand ran up and down her backside, grabbing one ass cheek and squeezing.

Before pulling his pants off, the man reached across her body and grabbed the clamps, giving them a little tug, which lit up Mandy's face. Simultaneous pain and pleasure. He whipped his cock out and slid it inside her after moving her panties to one side. The man spanked her hard. The clap sounded painful, but Mandy didn't seem to mind.

Christina noticed how big the man was before his cock disappeared inside Mandy's wet pussy. The man had a huge cock, which excited her. She hadn't been one to enjoy porn much, but watching it in real life was different. She liked this. The warm sensation started in her lower waist and quickly moved to her clit.

If Mandy's mouth weren't gagged, there would have been moans of pleasure, but it was hard to tell aside from garbles. The man drove into Mandy hard, slapping her ass again and again. He grunted as he plowed his pelvis into her. Occasionally, when the moment seemed right, he would reach over and grab the clamps. He would either pinch them or pull them, giving her a touch of pain. He looked down, measuring the distance to the whip and thought about getting it, but it was clear he didn't want to stop.

The man continued to thrust, pushing his cock inside, slamming his body against her mercilessly. Mandy continued to grunt through the gag. Mandy loved the powerless feeling. She loved constriction, and she loved someone else taking control. There was something about a touch of violence that did everything for Mandy, who was a masochist. She'd wished the man had gone further. She wanted him to use the candle wax and the plug.

After the man drilled Mandy for a long time, he stopped and pulled out of her. He soaked the floor with a squirt of cum. The man pulled away from Mandy and began to untie her. "What did you think?" he asked Christina.

"It looks like it could be fun," she agreed. She hadn't seen anything there that scared her. She wished she took the man up on his offer to join. She wasn't sure if she was a sub or not, but she was willing to find out. In the back of her mind, she thought she might be dominant because she could imagine herself being the one to inflict pain more than she could imagine herself being the one to receive.

"That was pretty good," Mandy said after the ball gag was removed from her mouth. "You should give it a try sometime. You won't regret it. The nipple clamps are probably my favorite toy in this room."

The man chuckled.

Out of curiosity, Christina took the clamp off her friend and lifted her shirt. She didn't mind them watching. There was nothing to be shy about now. She'd just watched them have the kinkiest sex she'd ever seen in her life. Christina clipped the clamp onto her nipple. It hurt at first, but when the pain began to subside, she understood. It felt amazing.

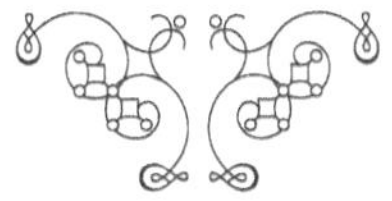

What Pleases Him Most

Thomas Kearnes

Each time Cutter and I went to the bathhouse, I shot through the halls of rented rooms, past the bank of grimy, oblong windows overlooking the outdoor pool, and through the steam room beside the hot tub. I needed to be numb. Cutter so enjoyed all the flesh on display, I couldn't refuse him. Occasionally, of course, I found a man to bring back to our room, but honestly, I would've been happy had Cutter been the only man beside me, loving me. Even with him near, I needed the tweak to keep me from stripping away my skin. Every time, part of me considered scrambling home, and every time, the rest of me remained paralyzed with desire. I could never leave our rented room.

Cutter and I sat on his bed, passing the pipe. Posters of great Greek landmarks covered his walls. A twittering bluejay outside his window distracted him, so I snuck another hit.

"Careful, boy." His gaze didn't leave the window. "Don't get so high you can't get hard."

I grinned, delighted to be caught. Cutter always found me out. Perhaps that was a condition of love. "Why do you think I'm always the catcher?" I asked.

"'Cause you like what I pitch."

I laughed and passed the pipe. Cutter was good to me. He volunteered his house in uptown Dallas for our weekends and occasional weeknights together. I still lived in a dorm with a nosy kid from the East Coast.

True, Cutter was thirty-seven, but I did my best not to think what would happen, how that age gap would bend and flex into something more obscene if we managed to stay together after these first few months. When he reached fifty, I would be thirty-three. These weekly trips to the Dallas Spa were the price of admission, I told myself, the cost of procuring a boyfriend as accomplished, sexy, and—well, *manly* as Cutter Drake.

"Just a few more hits," I said. "You know, to fortify me."

"You and your big words."

"I'm sorry, but that place … you know …"

He scooped the long end of the pipe into the tiny, plastic bag of tweak and ushered another rock into its mouth. "Yes, Darren, I'm aware of your feelings about the bathhouse."

My boyfriend was gorgeous, and I wasn't his only admirer. At the bathhouse, I watched the way men never stopped but turned their heads, keeping their eyes on Cutter as he passed. He had a fantastic body. He liked to call me from the 24-hour gym downtown to brag whenever he maxed more weight while working out. But it was his face, with the slim, sharp nose, the pale gray eyes, the long locks of rust-colored hair that flopped past his eyebrows, and the way his smile spread like melting butter—that was where I caught myself gazing whenever he was distracted. And best of all, he was a man—masculine and confident, not like those prissy, shaven boys trolling the sidewalks in Oak Lawn.

"I'm sorry." I meant it, but it didn't sound like I did.

"We don't have to go."

"You love it there."

"I love watching men fuck you."

I tried to smile. Granted, Cutter never forced any man on me. I got final approval on each trick. Always, at some point, as Cutter took snapshots with his smartphone, I began to drift. I thought about Cutter invading me after the stranger left, what he would say, how he would praise me, like a beloved pet. I did these things, these men, for him. Whenever I broke away from an encounter to look at him, however, I saw the pride, the lust in his eyes. I assured myself there was no higher calling than pleasing the man who loved me.

"It'll be just past four when we get there," I said. "We'll be hours ahead of the club crowd."

"Too many twinks at night. The guys in the afternoon are men."

"Like you," I said.

He pulled me close and kissed me so softly, I felt my heart drop into my stomach. Outside, the bluejay twittered again. I listened to its panicked cries as Cutter eased me down onto the bed. He set the pipe on the nightstand and eased his frame upon me. Perhaps we wouldn't make the bathhouse until five, or six, or later!

⁂

Cutter carried an old, black gym bag to the bathhouse. Inside were all the necessities for fucking strangers: lubricant, condoms, bottles of Gatorade, cock rings, a tweak pipe, and about an eight-ball of crystal. We strolled down Swiss Avenue, staring straight ahead.

Our first time there, Cutter had warned me it was considered impolite to make eye contact with men leaving the building. Frank appraisal only occurred in the halls, among the labyrinth of numbered rooms, or, sometimes, in the steam room and sauna. Basically, anywhere beyond the check-in desk was fair game. At the time, it didn't make sense, but I did as instructed, not acknowledging the gaze of a passing muscle guy.

Today, there was no one leaving when we arrived. Cutter joked with the skinny man behind the check-in counter. He flashed his credit card, then collected our room key and the white, threadbare towels. Our check-in complete, Cutter grandly swung out his arm to catch the swinging door. I chuckled at his mock chivalry.

We strolled through the lounge. It was very large, a pool table at one end and, at the other, an arrangement of couches and chairs before a big-screen television. Cutter once told me the men who frequented this room were either too ugly for sex or too wired to chase it. A Cameron Diaz movie played to the small group of bare-chested men seated around the set. My gaze fell on one of them. He was maybe forty, with a solid build. Coarse chest hair partially obscured his admirable physique. He swiveled his head, catching me as I stared. I averted my gaze, but Cutter noted our awkward exchange.

"Already on the prowl, boy?"

"No, I just … I thought I knew him."

"Probably saw him here before."

"I'm sure that's it." I forced my voice up an octave, like a stewardess instructing passengers how to save their own damn lives. I asked if he'd rented a VIP room.

"Follow me." Cutter grabbed my wrist, pulling me through the curved hallway that connected the lounge to the halls of rented rooms. We passed the stone archway leading to the hot tub, showers, and sauna. Cutter insisted I shower after sex, no matter how brief the encounter. Built into the stone hallway was a series of windows looking out over the kidney-shaped pool and stone sundeck. It was an overcast autumn day; no men occupied the deck chairs. As we entered the first hall, the awful staccato of electronic house music thumped over the speakers. I never understood gay men remixing perfectly good songs until one sounded like the next. In my intoxicated state, though, I found the steady bass soothing. I imagined Cutter penetrating me in time to the pulsing beat.

He led me down a small hallway with no doors on either side. He'd booked a VIP room after all! There were only three such rooms in the club, each complete with a queen-sized sheeted mattress, pillows, and a television bolted high on the wall, playing nonstop gay pornography. There was plenty of room to maneuver and play, unlike the regular rentals, which were the size of broom closets, the twin-sized rubber mattress taking up half the space.

While thrilled with our swank accommodations, a prick of fear settled at the base of my skull. Why shell out the cash for a VIP room unless he planned something exotic, something that did not arouse me? Various unpleasant scenarios flitted through my head. Cutter tossed his gym bag on the bed and began to strip.

"Hurry up and get undressed. We've gotta get your ass plowed."

I tried to laugh but instead produced a strange, sticky sound. Within minutes, some strange man would ram his shaft inside me, and I suddenly felt tired and slow, like expired gelatin. I didn't want to be here. I wasn't sure where I wanted to be instead, but my anxiety needed no specific locale.

"Been working out more?" Cutter glanced at my naked torso.

I shrugged and smiled shyly. At the moment, I couldn't remember whether I had.

"Your abs are getting more defined. Keep up the good work."

I rubbed my taut abdomen, doubting his praise.

Cutter pulled me into an embrace. "You're a very sexy boy, Darren Young."

He said it with such burnt-ember huskiness that I knew I'd consent to whatever he desired. I had friends who yearned for such grand compliments. I knew I was lucky—my luck had its own presence apart from us.

"You should find someone in no time," Cutter whispered into my ear.

I stripped and wrapped the towel around my waist. I was tempted to haggle for a little more tweak, but I didn't want to delay. He put much effort into these trips; in reality, my role was incidental.

I felt foolish, so I left the room. As instructed, I left the door cracked open so any passing man could glimpse Cutter stroking himself. After rotating my shoulders to loosen up, I looked both ways down the hall, wondering which way was best. One led back the maze's entrance, the other, into the depths. I had yet to pass any man, so I ventured further into the maze. The high floodlights dimmed as I ambled forward, the hallway finally opening into a wider hall, this one with closed doors on each side, all in a row. Actually, not every door was shut. I passed one room and saw inside a young, black man pleasuring himself, watching himself masturbate with stern concentration. He never noticed me. Cutter and I had an agreement: white men only.

A moment later, a young couple passed, their heads tilted together as if they exchanged military code. They were my age, and one of them—the brunet—was scalding hot, with a lithe, long body, mouth like an open cut in the skin. Both glanced at me, and I noted their haughtiness, these members of the Dallas Gay Mafia. You ran into these men everywhere in the Oak Lawn, the city's gay nexus. They dressed impeccably, with gym-toned bodies and beautiful, unblemished faces. They condemned anyone less fantastic with a sneer, including me. I wasn't unattractive. I studied myself in the mirror before every visit to the bathhouse, as if my looks might have soured overnight. These Mafia boys could make any man feel instantly worthless. I looked away. One laughed as they passed me. His boyfriend half-heartedly shushed him before laughing himself. I admired their brazen belief in their power to attract.

When searching for men, I simply circled the hallways until finding one. Men left rooms, returned from the showers or elsewhere, a steady tide of new faces. I noticed an older man, maybe forty-five, with a beer belly and graying fur matted on his shoulders. Next, I saw a scrawny kid who flashed me a gold-toothed smile that I adamantly ignored. There was a trio of men, each around thirty, in heated, hushed discussion, none of them gazing at me even when my arm brushed one of theirs. How long would I circle these halls? Some days, it could take fifteen minutes. Had anyone knocked on the door of our VIP room, taking the open door as an invitation? He might now be pounding some guy senseless. I didn't want to be here. I tried my luck elsewhere.

The hot tub was a brown-tiled, in-ground pool with rushing jets protruding from its walls, roiling the water, often just lukewarm. Today offered no surprise. I slipped off my towel and entered the water.

There were three other men in the pool, but my eyes locked on just one. He sat at the opposite end, absently waving his arms through the bubbles. He was perhaps thirty, with long, dirty blond hair hanging past his jawline. A wide, welcoming smile seemed in response to a private joke. I felt awkward, staring so long, but the man finally broke from his reverie and met my gaze. My God, such a smile!

"You're cute," I said. Excessive wit was just wasted breath.

"So are you."

I moved closer, the warm water thick around my hips and thighs. The man let me come closer. "You been partying?" I asked.

"Maybe. You got some more?"

"I never come without it." The gravity of that statement spooked me.

"Is it just you here? You come with a friend?"

"My boyfriend, Cutter."

"I wanna know *your* name." The man hesitantly pressed his palm against my chest.

"Darren," I said.

"So, your boyfriend likes threesomes?"

"Actually, he likes to watch hot guys fuck me."

His smile never faded, but his eyes narrowed. "What does he do while I'm pounding you?"

"He takes pictures."

A doubtful expression appeared. "You mean, for a website?"

"Oh, no, no, no. Just for our personal use." Then, I volunteered something I hadn't planned: "I think he jacks off to them when I'm not around."

His head snapped back, and a gasp of amusement wrenched loose. I hadn't believed it that funny, but I laughed too. When he laughed, whoever he was, you laughed with him.

"We're staying in one of the VIP rooms," I said. "You ever been inside one?"

"A few months ago." He smiled earnestly. I felt cheap. "Hope I live up to your boyfriend's expectations."

"You'll like Cutter. He just enjoys the show."

He told me his name was Raymond. I'd forgotten to ask. As we made our way to the VIP room, not speaking, I wondered how long I could've gone without knowing what to call him. I found the door still cracked. I eased it farther open. Cutter had dimmed the lights, so it took me a moment to make out his figure, stroking himself while onscreen moans filled the room.

"Looks like he may be busy," Raymond muttered.

"He was waiting," I replied, equally quiet. Then, louder, I called out, "I brought company!"

Cutter bolted upright and smiled. Whether it was meant exclusively for me, I couldn't tell. Cutter rose from the bed and asked him if I'd informed him of our situation. He didn't bother with the towel. He extended his hand to Raymond.

"Didn't tell me how hot you'd be," our guest replied.

"I'm not the main attraction."

"Where should we start?" Raymond blithely tossed his white towel onto the stone floor.

"Kiss him for now," my boyfriend instructed. "Move slowly."

Raymond theatrically slapped his hands together. He then slid them around my waist and gently pulled me into his arms. "I can go slow," he murmured, more for me than Cutter.

He kissed me. Every time a new man kissed me, I compared his kiss to Cutter's. The strangers' kisses were rarely better, but Raymond knew how to flutter his thick, plump lips effortlessly over my mouth. After a few moments, the tip of his tongue pushed its way through my lips. I allowed it entry. Our kiss deepened. Cutter watched in silence. As my head teetered back and forth under the force of the kiss, I caught a brief glance at my boyfriend. He stood motionless, his smartphone loosely held. This was unusual. Typically, Cutter couldn't wait to start shooting. Worry distracted me from Raymond's commanding kiss, but he didn't seem to notice. Cutter snapped out of his daze and aimed the phone. He snapped several shots in a row, never changing position. Raymond's hands grew bolder. The towel remained snug around my hips. Through the fabric, Raymond's desire couldn't be ignored.

"Darren," Cutter called, his voice soft. Raymond wouldn't stop kissing me.

"What?" I asked breathlessly.

"Suck his cock."

"Now?"

"Yeah, man. I wanna see that shit right now."

"Sounds good," Raymond said. He then added in a softer voice, "If that's all right with you, buddy."

Raymond was a handsome man. His face had yet to register the smile lines and slight crow's feet that Cutter's face held. There was a slight gap between his two front teeth. He instinctively bowed his head whenever he smiled. His eyes were a dazzling cornflower blue.

"Sure," I replied, easing down to my knees.

I slid him between my lips, allowing him to surge all the way to the back of my throat. My head bobbed, oddly in sync with the moans on the TV. Raymond's moans joined them, filling the room.

"Good boy," muttered Cutter, raising the smartphone to his face. "That's a good boy."

Raymond tasted fantastic. I felt the wild charge I always felt knowing I could bring a man that intense a pleasure. You could go mad with the power. And there was my boyfriend, the man I loved, clicking away with his phone.

The first time Cutter showed me the photos of a bathhouse encounter, he sequenced them out upon the bedspread, beaming like a proud father. "You look hot in that one, boy," he said. And then, "I thought he was going to scream when you moved your ass like that." And then, "I'm gonna have to watch you closely, or you'll run off to the porn studio."

I felt nothing looking at these graphic images. Because of the tweak, I rarely remembered performing these acts, but I played along, pantomiming bashfulness or pride, whatever reaction Cutter wanted. I knew that, for him, this part was just as important as the sex itself, if not more so. He urged me to keep a snapshot or two, but I always refused. These were for him, I said. He believed me.

Back in the VIP room, while Raymond gently thrust his hips, sending himself deeper down my throat, I heard a man wail in the distance. I thought it had to be the porn, but this sounded more like a cry of anguish. Also, it definitely came from just outside the closed door. Neither Raymond nor Cutter made any expression to indicate they'd heard it, so I resumed my task. But then the same cry came, only louder.

"What the fuck was that?" Cutter asked.

We heard it again, this time trailing off into a series of jagged sobs.

Even Raymond broke from his bliss. "Is some guy out there crying?"

I stopped sucking and turned to the door. Cutter crossed the room, opening it. From my position on the floor, I couldn't see what the other two saw. But then, a young man staggered through the doorway and dropped to his knees before us. His thin, bony shoulders shook, and his arms enveloped his narrow chest. His face contorted in bereavement. While Cutter stood still in front of him, our intruder sobbed and sobbed.

Finally, Raymond spoke. "Dude, what the fuck happened?"

The crying man tried to speak, but no words came. Milky snot ran from his nose and over his lips, glistening in the dim light. He tried to speak again.

Cutter gently placed a hand on his shoulder. "Are you here with someone?" he asked, showing a compassion that surprised me, though I don't know why. Cutter had shown me kindness countless times. I didn't want to be here. "Can we get you something?"

The man settled down and sank onto the floor, bottom resting on the soles of his feet. He wore only a white towel around his hips. *Just like us*, I thought. *He might be just like us.*

"I'm with Jerry," he moaned.

"Is that your boyfriend?" Cutter asked.

"I don't think so," the man stammered. "At least, not anymore!" He began to howl.

I tore my gaze away from the wreckage to check on Raymond. His features had darkened, his once ample mouth shut tightly, the lips thin and severe. He glared at the poor man through slit eyelids. His arms folded tightly over his chest. I turned back to Cutter and the crying man as he tried to help the man to his feet.

"Let's go find Jerry," Cutter said.

"He doesn't want me anymore."

"I'm sure that's not true. C'mon, let's go."

"No! No! It is true! He found some piece of ass at the hot tub! Goodbye, Keith!" His hand fluttered away from him as if trying to escape.

"That's your name?" Cutter asked. "Keith?"

Keith moaned and nodded. He rubbed furiously at his eyes. By then, Cutter had maneuvered the intruder back toward the doorway. Believing the situation almost contained, I returned my attention to Raymond, but he was grabbing his towel from the floor. The brisk strokes he made wrapping it around his waist unnerved me. Only minutes ago, we'd been kissing like long-time lovers, like … Cutter and I might.

"You don't have to leave," I said.

"Sorry, man, that was kind of a buzzkill."

Raymond stomped through the door. Cutter and the crying man had already gone outside. I stood there, helpless. I wondered if any of Cutter's snapshots were angled to capture Raymond's lovely face. More likely, they were focused solely on my lips gliding back and forth upon his shaft. That's what my boyfriend wanted to remember: how I looked giving another man pleasure.

The door clicked shut. I glanced down and saw my swollen excitement begin its retreat beneath my towel. This flood of disappointment surprised me. Other candidates were stalking the halls. All I had to do was wait for Cutter, and then leave to find them. When the pursuit reached its fever pitch, I let myself get carried away on the adrenaline.

Still, I needed something to numb myself further, to guarantee no doubts would descend. I hurried to the side of the bed and opened Cutter's gym bag. I rifled through it, looking for the bag of tweak. Just a couple of hits, that's all I needed. After locating the pipe wrapped inside a sock, I loaded it with a sizable crystal only to realize I'd yet to locate a lighter. I ransacked the bag once again but had no luck. He worried about how much I smoked. Defeated, I sank onto the bed and listlessly watched the screen as one man penetrated another. I couldn't help wondering whether Raymond and I would have moved with comparable precision.

After a few moments, I slid off the bed, slipped the loaded pipe back into the gym bag, and made my way for the door. Even though being alone in the VIP room meant I was spared the glares of the strange men lurking outside, it also meant I had no distraction from the rot and doom I felt in this dank fuck factory.

Just a month ago, I'd spent the night with a man I met while at my cousin's wedding in Tyler. He was big and charming and insatiable. I forgot, at least for a few moments, that Cutter was in Dallas, waiting for me. What if Cutter asked me to do something I simply couldn't stomach? Would he leave me stranded with damp sheets and faded semen stains on the walls?

"My God, some people are so fucking needy!" Cutter burst through the door. He crossed the room with a long, energetic stride.

"Did you ever find his boyfriend?"

"I asked his room number, but the guy flat-out refused to go back. You won't believe what happened next." The two men in the porn increased their volume and urgency. Cutter shook his head and smacked his palm against his forehead. "Anyway, we're standing near the hot tub, and he grabs my junk, says he want to fuck. We could rent a separate room, his treat."

"Oh, my God," I said with a flat affect. It was always painful to be reminded of this: Cutter was a devastatingly gorgeous man. Of course, other men desired him. And there was no guarantee they'd desire me too.

"I just looked at him and said—and you should've heard how I said it. I looked him dead in the eye and said, 'I have a boyfriend, you dumb faggot.'" Making that declaration, he sounded like a no-nonsense sheriff from an old sitcom.

I didn't fight the warmth I felt spreading through me after he said that. "What did he say?" I rose to my knees on the bed.

"He just shrugged, shook his head, and said, 'Your loss.' I guess he's still looking for dick."

"What a loser!" I cried.

"No shit. Maybe we shouldn't have come here today."

I couldn't keep the enthusiasm out of my tone. "You mean you're ready to leave?"

Cutter rounded the bed and stopped. I was still on my knees atop the mattress, so our heads were level. He caressed my cheek. He held my gaze for so long, I forgot about Raymond's electric blue eyes. Yes, there were other desirable men in the world, in this very building, but Cutter Drake had chosen me. *Me*. Whatever I had to endure to keep his love would be endured—enjoyed!

⁂

I was exhausted and sweating like a sow in the mid-August sun. I lay beside him, the sheets askew from our thrashing. I listened to Cutter's breath and slowed mine until it fell into rhythm with his. It took me a bit to realize he'd spoken.

"You wanna run outside and grab me a water?" he asked.

"Don't you have Gatorade in your bag?"

"Yeah, but water sounds better."

"I'm so fucking whipped right now," I moaned.

"I'll suck your dick," Cutter said.

I rose to my side and looked at him, hoping he could see my merriment. "You should do that because you love me."

"I'll love you more when I'm hydrated."

I carried a limp dollar in my fist for the drink machine. More than anything, I wished I could make the trek to the lobby without passing any other man. I was done with men for that day, every man except Cutter. I turned the corner and headed out of the maze.

I only saw two men in the hot tub and another three watching the lounge television as I hurried past. None of them noticed me. I slid the dollar into the drink machine and pushed the correct button. Just as I bent over to retrieve the jettisoned bottle, a figure in a white towel appeared beside me.

"You better be grateful he loves you."

Alarmed, I swiftly glanced over my shoulder and saw Keith glaring at me. His eyes were still red and bleary.

"What did you say to me?"

"You heard me the first time."

I gulped. "Cutter told me what you did."

Keith's stance softened. He hitched up one shoulder in defiance. "You know how hot he is—you're the one he's taking home."

"I have to get back to the room," I stammered, abruptly turning to leave. Keith followed me, his wide strides matching my own. I didn't want to be here.

"You think some kid can keep him happy for long?"

"Stop following me!" One of the men watching television turned to see the commotion.

"If he really wanted just you, he wouldn't bring you here."

"I don't wanna talk to you."

We had reached the windowed hallway connecting the lounge to the maze. Keith seized my shoulder and spun me around. I couldn't remember the last time a man looked at me with such hate, and I knew he wished me dead. My only crime was being loved and returning that love.

"I'm not giving up, kid," he said. "Men like him get bored with little boys. Remember that."

I nodded dumbly and backed away. I bumped into a wrought-iron table and jumped at the screech the table leg made dragging on the floor. Recovering, I ran into the maze, fully expecting Keith to follow. But when I reached the hallway leading to our VIP room, he was gone. Taking a moment to collect myself before joining Cutter—I couldn't tell him about this, never!—I felt hot tears stinging the corners of my eyes. I pawed at them, ashamed. Taking a deep breath, I turned the doorknob.

"What took you so long, boy?"

"There was more than one brand of water," I said.

"That's bullshit. I don't care what the label says, water is fucking water."

He grabbed the drink and unscrewed the lid. Knowing I was giving myself away, I stared at my boyfriend, as if trying to memorize his face before he vanished among these rented rooms and rented desires.

"Boy, what's wrong?"

"Please, let's go home!"

I felt the tears slide down my cheeks. I buried my face in my hands. The shakes my body made as I cried left no doubt that I needed my man to comfort me—right now.

Cutter embraced me. "Baby, it's all right. I didn't know this place upset you that much."

"It does, it does."

He tried to laugh. "C'mon, boy, you're not supposed to cry in a bathhouse."

"What can you do here?"

My boyfriend, the man I loved, smiled. "This," he said and pressed his mouth over mine.

With that, I was silenced. Through the speakers, an insistent bassline pounded. The boys on television groaned and grunted. Cutter pulled his face away. He gazed into my eyes. Did he want me to do something? I couldn't remember the last time I'd seen that look, so I simply smiled, awaiting his next desire.

Contributors

E. W. Farnsworth

E. W. Farnsworth is widely published online and in print. For further information on the author and his works, please see **www.ewfarnsworth.com**.

Philippe Marron

Philippe Marron, an author in Baltimore, has published textbooks and a subversive political thriller.

Chimera is based on the true story of a visit to a sex club in San Francisco.

Shanjida Nusrath Ali

Shanjida first started writing on Wattpad. Then with the love and support of her readers, she self-published her first book, *Destroyed* (Dark Love Due#1). Meanwhile, when she's not writing, Shanjida spends her free time reading books or improving her art skills.

She currently lives in Bangladesh with her family, and is completing her studies in English Language and Art.

Thomas Kearnes

Thomas Kearnes graduated from the University of Texas at Austin with an MA in film writing. His fiction has appeared in Gulf Coast, Berkeley Fiction Review, Timber, Hobart, Gertrude, A cappella Zoo, Split Lip Magazine, Cutthroat, Litro, PANK, BULL: Men's Fiction, Gulf Stream Magazine, Wraparound South, Night Train, 3:AM Magazine, Word Riot, Storyglossia, Driftwood Press, Adroit Journal, The Matador Review, Pseudopod, Underbelly Magazine, Black Dandy, the Best Gay Stories series, Mary: A Journal of New Writing, wigleaf, SmokeLong Quarterly, Pidgeonholes, Sundog Lit, The Citron Review, and elsewhere. He is a three-time Pushcart Prize nominee and three-time Best of the Net nominee. Originally from East Texas, he now lives near Houston and works as an English tutor at a local community college. His debut collection of short fiction, "Texas Crude" is now available at Lethe Press, Amazon and Barnes & Noble.

Wolfgang Domino

Wolfgang Domino is passionate about writing erotica. He lives in the woods of Maine, enjoys chess, cycling and reading.

Some of his work has appeared on Myerotica.com and Literotica.com. Wolfgang is currently working on a novella he hopes to finish sometime next year.

Other Works from Temptation Press

Summer Fling

Kiss & Tell

The Professor

Private Lessons

Choices

This Sub's for You

Intimate Moments

Forbidden

The Boss

A Note from the Publisher

How to Thank a Contributor

Dear Reader,

Everyone at Temptation Press would like to thank you for reading *Nights in the City: An Erotic Collection*. If you would like to thank a particular contributor, the best way is to leave a review for them. You may do so by leaving one on our Goodreads page, under the title, *Nights in the City*, by using the link below:

http://www.goodreads.com/TemptationPress

and be sure to mention the contributor directly.

Why should you leave a review? Reviews help budding authors build their credibility in the book industry. By posting a review on Goodreads and other review sites, you help other readers find new authors they may wish to follow, and you never know, your review may end up on an author's website one day.

⁂

Friend us on Goodreads:
https://www.goodreads.com/TemptationPress

Visit our website:
http://www.TemptationPress.com